IT WAS RAIN

It Was Rain

Leecia Clinkscales

To order additional copies of this book, contact:
Xlibris
1-888-795-4274
www.Xlibris.com
Orders@Xlibris.com
769330

Leecia Clinkscales is a 18-year old college student. Youngest of 3, Leecia graduated from Mckinley highschool and is now attending Daemen, a Private college in Buffalo NY.

She started writing poetry at the age of 10 but always wanted something more. To tell a story, indulge in a different life. So, with that she began playing with creative writing. Thinking of short stories, and, eventually thought of a completely original plot. Aspiring to be a successful author, Leecia is determined to put her name on the map no matter which way she does it.

I always relive the moment that the reality I made came crashing down around me. I could hear my heart thumping. Making it hard for me to hear...to breathe. I remember the silence in my head, for the first time there was no whispering, laughing, or angry voices. There were no flashbacks of distant faces or muffled music. All I remember hearing was the officers screaming such profane things like, my life wasn't really mine.

Detective Grayson was cleanest cut man I'd ever seen. He had skin like caramel and arms that looked so warm and protecting, but his eyes were like darts to a target. His voice was deep. It could stop any and everyone in their tracks, and leave them stuck, just like me.

"Your name is Cassie Powers. Your parents are Carson and Chasity Powers. Everyone thought you were killed in a car accident with your parents, but you were kidnapped by Martin Tucker."

The words spilled from his mouth like he tried to process it himself. It was the truth... My life had been taken from me once, and I recollected that. I just couldn't believe they would try to take away another. My voice cracked as I plead my case.

"My name is Kori Tucker, and Martin Tucker is my father, he's alive and well… I'd like to go home now, please."

My head felt heavy, like the thoughts that raced through my mind had cinderblock shoes on. By then I had my mind set on avoiding saying the truth out loud. I refused to make this real. I refused to accept my fate.

Officer Grayson didn't care about what I wanted, so the profane words spewed out like word vomit.

"What did Mr. Tucker tell you about your mother?"

I quickly snapped back,

"My mother died at child birth"

I forced my burning, lying tears out of my eyes, down my cheek, and watched them disappear into the fabric of my pants. My heart stopped thumping. Gone with it, werethe quiet thoughts. The ones that returned were angry, or maybe just concerned. These thoughts were also distant cries from the woman I wouldn't... couldn't admit was once real.

"You know the truth buttercup, tell our story."

I heard over and over. Fighting the urge to slap my hands against my ears to try and drown the taunting voice out. I just laid my head down. Detective Grayson sung a satisfied, and sarcastic tune when he said

"Tired of denying?"

when he got no reply he left me there, alone. Finally, I could think and process the pros and cons of accepting the truth. What I'd be leaving behind... who I would be leaving behind. The man who, in my eyes gave me a life to remember... A life I had no choice but to remember...

I had a pretty good life. I lived in the sunshine state, Tampa Bay Florida. My dad was around 6'0, light skinned and had a bit of meat on him. He had a serious face 90% of the time, I was surprised he didn't have worry lines on his forehead. He had hazel eyes and a hairless face, he always kept his hair cut with a fade on the side. There was never a time we went out together when a woman didn't try to snatch him up or throw herself at him. I was bonus points for him, a single dad? That was on every woman's list of conquests and definitely hard to find. I wish dad and I were thick as thieves. I tried to picture a life where I was actually close to him. Whenever someone asked I told them we played music, hit all the tones in our favorite musicals too. We played catch, went to the park, chased birds and attempted to skip rocks. He never freaked out when it was time to buy bras, teach me about my period or talk about boys. He was mom, dad, aunt and all my cousins to me because that's what I wanted him to be.

I did have my uncle Aaron though. His last name was Sanders so I just called him "uncle Sandy" for short. He called me "K crazy". We were always good at nicknames and making each other feel better. I would tell him about my long day at school and he would tell me about his hard day at work. He was better at putting a smile on my face than I was. He used to tell the worst stories and say "see, you could be bad at everything, even telling bed time stories like me, but you're not, you're more amazing than I could've imagined, even from your pictures." I never knew what he meant by that but I didn't care, to him I was the best. My uncle Sandy was taller than my dad, so around 6'3, he had light brown eyes and fine features. He had a small beard and connecting sideburns. His shoulders were very broad, I loved to sit on them so I could see the world. He was strong and had a deep voice, whenever he said something I would reach up to feel the vibrations in his neck. I would try to make my voice just like his, it never worked though.

He would usually be around whenever my dad wasn't, so I never had a nanny, never really played outside, and from kinder-garden to 9th grade I went to a small private school. My home was my outlet and playground for a huge portion of my life. The outside has white and grey brick, it's moderately big, four bedrooms, two and a half bathrooms. We have a large front yard with sprinklers and of course gargoyles. The inside is laid with black leather furniture, crème colored carpet and gorgeous paintings. Flat screens in every room besides the bathroom, but there are heated floors and walk in showers. My room was the second biggest out of them all. I have gray and yellow stripped walls, a king sized bed with a black sparkled canopy. I have a huge TV stand right in front and "for show" dressers on each side. I have a walk in closet, not too big but, it's enough to long for if I didn't have it. The 2 extra rooms used to be in use until I grew up and no longer needed a play room, and we never really have guests so I guess theextra bed in there goes to use when my uncle spends the night. I switched from my old play room to throwing parties for myself in our finished basement, it has a pool and fuse ball table. A few couches and bean bag chairs, a bar I was never allowed to even sit in front of, but it was a nice escape.

I can't remember the last time I was in my father's room, the door is always closed and when it is open he's standing in front of it. When I was in the house playing alone I remember picturing an evil lair or a secret wonderland hidden behind the doors. I had such an imagination, I had no choice being the only child. I spent my entire freshman and sophomore year at a private high school and I hated every minute of it. The girls were snotty and all the guys were childish. Imagine my relief when, after a summer of begging, my dad let me go to a public high school.

As soon as I walked into Chasity high I was determined to make the next two years of my life memorable. Having all my time spent in the marble hallways, catching the bus with gossiping girls, backstabbing friends, athletic stars, academic over-achievers and people just like me, normal. Since the weather was always warm people continuously left the house in their best. Chasity high was known for the rich and disturbingly perfect people with considerable academic upstanding. There's four floors, all designated for grades 9-12. High school is exactly how I pictured it to be, busy, colorful, intense…I made so many friends in my first couple of days. A few enemies too. By my junior year I was still only 5'0, I had hair that made it down to the small of my back, no more awkwardness to my walk, braces or pimples. I was very glad I went through puberty earlier that year. My dad or Uncle Sandy weren't too happy about that though. I had a little pudge to my stomach but it fit my thighs and butt well, barely any cleavage, but a C cup was ok. I guess I was considered pretty since all the cheerleaders hated me and jocks loved me. Disregarding the rest of them, I was into the face of the Chasity high athletic teams, Antonio Rivet. He kept his hair cut short with a crisp edge up. His clear and milk chocolate like skin, pearly white teeth and big arms flowed so perfectly together, he had me completely stuck on him. I wasn't looking at anybody else. He was 19, and a senior though, so I don't think he would've noticed me unless I made him. I made my best friend the 10th day of school. It was a Wednesday, September 12th 2002 around 11:00 in 4th period when she commented my shoes. I know, very cliché, but I looked down to realize they were the same. I laughed, she laughed, so we sat next to each other. It was chemistry, with Mr. Kannon. He was a big man with broad, hunched over shoulders, a half bald head, with a gray and black mustache. He had a voice as if he had a cold 365 days a year, but he told thecorniest jokes I've ever heard, so it was my favorite class of the day. Before class started I'd forgotten to ask her name, so I found out when attendance rolled around. Kylah Jackson. White, long red haired, big blue eyed, freckled face, 4'11, curvy, stop traffic smile Kylah Jackson. She would be my best friend, I knew it. Right before the bell we compared schedules, we had study hall, gym, and English together, they were all last periods of the day. We exchanged numbers and I went our separate ways.

It was my first time actually going into the lunch room, I had a couple associates that walked in with me though. Ashanti, Lora and Gabe, just some people that I got grouped with first period. I wasn't worried about them. I was too busy trying to find Antonio. Trying to look through the cafeteria that seemed to be half the size of a football field. Finally, I found Antonio… His face glowed all the way from across the room, I almost got caught staring. Before Haley Price, the captain of the cheer team could grab the last seat next to him, I put my bag down and put on the nicest, calmest voice I could and said

"Is anybody sitting here?"

I got a smile. Me, Kori Tucker, a junior and a new face at Chasity, got a smile from Antonio, the star among stars for the athletic group.

"Of course, you didn't even have to ask. Your name is Kori right?"

He said with a deep voice that made me melt. "How did he know my name?"

I thought to myself. I was screaming and dancing in my head.

"Yeah, Antonio right? Star of the football, basketball, and track team, right?"

The biggest senior in the school was Duke Redon, and he thought I was just hilarious.

"You got yourself a fan there Toni! Let me know your secrets so I can get a fine joint like her."

I couldn't hide my rosy red cheeks, but I don't think Antonio found that too amusing.

"Yo, man chill out. She's beautiful, not a piece of meat. Plus, you could never be like me."

My eyes were wide open at that point. I hadn't expected him to be… a gentleman?

"Sorry about that Kori, you know us upper classman… But you look different."

I wasn't sure what to say, if I should laugh say thank you, ask what it meant to be different. Only thing that could come out of my mouth was,

"How'd you know my name?"

He chuckled and said

"I know all the girl's names"

and gave me a nudge on my arm. "Oh."

I said looking down at the nasty peas and sweet potato fries on my plate.

"Hey I'm just messing with you, I saw you walking down the hall with Kylah, asked her what your name was, I'm friends with her boyfriend. You stopped me in my tracks girl."

I felt a huge wave of relief…

"She's the first cool girl I've met since school started. You caught my eye too by the way, I saw your name on your binder though."

I tried to sound as cool as possible.

"Take my number down, and let me get yours. I probably won't see you again today. Hopefully I do though."

I grabbed a piece of paper and put my number down. I tried to write my numbers as pretty as numbers could look. He slid me a piece of paper with his name and number on it. He pulled out his phone and said

"Take a picture with me K. I'm going to call you K for short."

I giggled and fixed my hair, got closer to smile and he wrapped his arm around me... He smelt like a bunch of candy and butterscotch. After this moment nobody could tell me he wasn't perfect. He smiled as big as me and said

"Ok one more. I hope you don't mind."

I didn't know what I would mind until he kissed me on my cheek. My hands flew to my face to hide my huge smile and blushing cheeks. He said with a laugh,

"I'm definitely using this one as your contact picture."

I jokingly rolled my eyes and grabbed my books as the bell rung and disappeared in the crowd. I could feel him watching me walk away, but I didn't look back.

I saw Kylah in the hallway, before I could get anything out she said

"GUESS WHO ASKED ABOUT YOU!"

in a squeaky voice, bouncing up and down.

"Actually, don't even guess because I'm going to tell you! It was Antonio Rivet! The athlete star! He told me you were cute, and asked me what your name was. EEEEEEEEEP. This also gives me an excuse to invite you over today. You down?"

I took a deep breath, knowing I wouldn't breath for a while when I tell her about what happened in the café.

"I asked him if I could sit next to him, he was flirting, I gave him my number, he gave me his, He KISSED my cheek in one of the pictures we took and he said that it would be my contact picture. He even gave me a nickname! It's "K" I played it cool but he totally watched me walk away."

We both bounced up and down, not even realizing the bell was about to ring. Kylah said

"I got to see you later so I can get more details!"

I skipped down the hall and said

"I'm going to text my dad and ask if I can come over!"

I wasn't sure if she heard me but as soon as I got into Health I texted him.

"Hey dad, I'm having the best day ever, I met a new friend, her name is Kylah and she asked me to come over today. Can I go? Pretty please, please, please."

I waited and waited for what felt like hours waiting for a reply, and then it came.

"Sure sweet pea, I'll take you when you get home. Now learn something!"

I was so excited I couldn't wait until the day ended. It was only 6th period, I had two more to go until I had anymore classes with Kylah. Then my phone vibrated again.

"Hey its Antonio, I hope this is K, I'd be sad if you gave me the wrong number lol. Save mine. See you around girl."

My smile went from one ear to the other, I couldn't concentrate at all for Health, Science or Math. 9th period rolled around and I have the study hall with Kylah, I couldn't wait to get there.

Walking to my study hall I was so wrapped up in thinking about Antonio that I didn't even see Haley walking down the hall. She bumped me so hard my books almost fell.

"Hey! What's your problem?"

I yelled, she just flipped her hair and continued walking with her posy of under clothed followers.

"Whatever."

I just kept walking. Getting into the study hall, my eyes jumped to see Duke Redon, the biggest senior in the school. He wouldn't even look at me after what happened in lunch. I was hoping I'd see Antonio, but I didn't. I didn't see Kylah either. The bell rung so I just took my seat and put my head down. Kylah came in a few minutes later with 2 pieces of pizza and cake.

"We had a little celebration in my math class, I wanted to spread the cheer."

I sat up straight and grabbed a napkin from the desk next to me.

"We need to go on a mission"

I said with the most serious voice I could muster up.

"I need to know everything I can about Haley Price."

Kylah giggled.

"Okay, well I can start your search off right. Her and Antonio used to date from their freshman year all the way up to this summer. I heard he broke up with her after she tried to get with my boyfriend, chase. Before me of course but he totally ratted her out. Then after the breakup she had a weird break down later for like 3 weeks. I don't know if that had to do with Antonio, but it is a coincidence."

I huffed and rolled my eyes. I don't understand why she would hate me like it's my fault they broke up. I didn't even know they were alive at the time.

"So she's mad because I'll treat him better right?"

Kylah and I both shared a laugh and just chilled out together the last three periods of the day.

I didn't see Antonio until dismissal, when he texted me and said "Turn around". I looked back and there he was, smiling like there were cameras everywhere.

"So you'll treat me better huh?"

I had no idea what he was referring to until it clicked, Ugh!

"Duke Redon!"

I shouted aloud, forgetting where I was. Antonio laughed and shook his head.

"You've been laughing at me all day."

I said blushing and looking away.

"It was just a joke that I was telling because Kylah told me what happened with you and Haley, after our little encounter in the hallway."

Then all of a sudden his smile stopped.

"If she talks to you, touches you, anything, let me know. Okay?"

I just shrugged my shoulders and looked around the halls for Kylah.

"Oh yeah, do you want a ride? I told Kylah and Chase I would take them home. You can ride in the front seat."

I grabbed my bag off the floor and nudged to tell him to come on. He grabbed my hand and I pulled back, just a little before I realized what was happening.

"I've never held anybody's hand before, just my dad and uncle... It feels... Nice."

He chuckled.

"You really are different... I'm glad I could be your first, hopefully not only at this."

I just ignored that comment. I never thought about anything like that before. The car ride home was nice, he had a decked out silver Jeep. I was going to go to Kylah's house first but I forgot my dad wanted to see me. When He pulled up to my house, Antonio gave me another peck, but strangely enough my dad was standing on the porch. I got out the car and he said

"Is that the friend?"

I looked back to see if Antonio had pulled off, but he didn't, of course he would be sitting there texting.

My dad charged to the front door, I tried to put my hands in front to stop him, but he's stronger than I am. He knocked hard on the window, Antonio dropped his phone and quickly rolled down the window. I jumped in front of my dad and said

"Excuse my father."

Antonio's eyes jumped open and he got out the car.

"Hi, my name is Antonio Rivet, I'm a senior at Chasity. H-how are you, sir?"

He said with the shakiest voice ever.

"Dad, please, let him be."

He bust out in a roar of laughter.

"What's up man, don't be so nervous. I knew who you were as soon as you pulled up, I know your father. Kareem Rivet, right?"

Antonio let off a long sigh of relief.

"Yes sir, that's my father, how do yawl know each other?"

My dad waved for him to follow him inside but I quickly intervened,

"Dad! You're supposed to be taking me to Kylah's house, remember?"

I said pulling his arm in the opposite direction. Antonio said

"I'm going over to..."

I quickly put my index finger up to my lips, I did not want my dad to know he would be over there. He continued,

"Actually, my mom did want me to babysit April." My dad shrugged his shoulders and said

"We just know each other from high school, but come on sweet pea, we can go now."

I ran over to hug Antonio, he lifted me off my feet and swung me around, I'm so glad my dad went to grab his keys. It was fun at Kylah's house, especially watching movies cuddled up with Antonio. I couldn't wait to be his girlfriend, start spending the night with Kylah so we can get closer, and get used to high school life. Everything was going so good... It could only go up from there... Right?

CHAPTER 2

The end of the first marking period was around the corner now, so all you see around school are kids running to guidance, and asking for passes to see teachers for extra credit. Me on the other hand, I was always good at school so it was all humorous to me. Kylah was failing history. It is one of my best subjects but I had no idea how to teach it. In the beginning of the year, I was offered a class in English 3 prep, a subject Antonio was horrible at. So, when after school tutoring rolled around I didn't mind going with Kylah because I got to tutor Antonio. It was October 12th when he asked me out, in his truck, with roses and a long letter. Who knew he was the romantic type. It's November 12th now, so you can say we're still in the cupcake stage and can't stand to be apart. Kylah was so cute with her boo. I was glad we became friends too. His name was Chase Monti, tall, slim, skin like milk chocolate. He has curly hair but a nice "fade" or whatever the boys call it. He wore a lot of jewelry too. His voice was deep but soft. He was like an invert, which is weird because Kylah is such an outgoing person, but they do say opposites attract. Chase is on the basketball team with Antonio though, so I guess he has to have somewhat of an outgoing side too. I'll just have to wait to see it.

On my way out the door to get on the bus after school, I heard a few short honks. I turn around to see if it was anybody I knew, to my surprise it was my Uncle Sandy. He had untightened his tie, unbuttoned the top buttons of his shirt and had a towel over his neck, so I knew he had a long day at work. I waved to let him know I knew he was there, then turned to see if I could find Antonio, but I couldn't, so I just skipped over to the car. When I was getting in the front seat I saw a pink sparkly bag in the back, so I climbed in and, of course, went to grab it. My uncle smacked my hand

"Stop being nosey. It's not for you."

I knew it was, so I just giggled and turned the radio up. It was our favorite song. We both sang loud

"IF YOU WEREN'T MY BESTFRIEND, I WOULDN'T KNOW WHAT TO DO, 'CAUSE I'LL NEVER LIVE WITHOUT YOUUUUUUUUU, THE CLOUDS AND THE MOON, DON'T GO TOGETHER LIKE ME AND YOUUUUUUUUU."

We both know it was corny, but we always bust out in a roar of laughter after we sang it.

"So how was your day K Crazy, I heard you got yourself a little boyfriend."

I blushed so hard, I couldn't believe my dad would tell him that,

"I was going to tell you!"

I shouted in a disappointed tone, uncle Sandy laughed,

"I actually didn't know, but I do now. So who's my first victim in the Kori's dating list?"

I rolled my eyes and said with the softest voice

"He's the most amazing guy in the world."

I threw my hands around in a circle, for dramatic affect. Uncle made a puking noise just to annoy me.

"Well, there goes my lunch. I'm still your favorite guy though right?"

He was parked in our driveway, so I jumped out and yelled back

"Saved by the bell."

I walked into an empty house. I had no idea where my dad was, I just shrugged my shoulders and went to the kitchen. Uncle Sandy followed, carrying that big pink bag.

"What are you carrying around in that bag that isn't for me?"

I said sarcastically.

"Open it and find out."

Uncle said placing the bag on the table. I threw all the extra paper on the floor, and to my surprise, my 36-year-old uncle sandy, got me something cute. It was my favorite brand, a Runway black and red dress, with a sweat suit, blanket and purse. I have no idea why it was such contradicting things in there.

"What is this for Uncle?"

I said confused, but when I looked up, it was Antonio, with flowers and a huge smile.

"What is this?" I said, trying to keep cool from all the excitement.

"It's our first date, I'm taking you out to dinner, which is why you have the dress, then we're going to the drive in to see a scary movie, hence the sweats, it's supposed to be chilly tonight."

I took the flowers and kissed him on the cheek. Only because Uncle sandy was around.

"What made you do this?"

"Well, I wanted to show you how committed I was, and I might have heard you tell Kylah that you've never been on a date."

I laughed and jumped into his arms

"Well thank you baby, I'm very excited."

He swung me around a few times then put me down and said

"I'll be back around 8:30, look gorgeous like I know you always do."

He gave me a kiss and left. I danced around the house, and went to try on my dress, I took pictures and sent them to Kylah.

"Why do I have the best boyfriend in the world, I must've be the nicest person in another life."

She texted me back excited, but she was with her boyfriend so she said she'd call me later. 7:00 rolled around and I began getting ready, my dad strolled past my room, into his and closed the door. I didn't want to bother him because he's not the best when he's angry, I just hoped Uncle sandy would talk to him. I finished curling my hair, and putting eye liner and mascara on. I even grabbed a little blush just because, I put on the necklace my dad said was my mother's before she died, she wore it on their first date, so I figured it'd be appropriate. I slipped on my black high heels, my gold ring, bracelets and favorite pair of hoop earrings, the black clutch purse that was in the bag Antonio gave me and was ready to go. I still had a bit of time left, so I decided to take a chance and talk to my dad. When I arrived at the door, I heard him and Sandy arguing, it was a low tone but I could hear bits and pieces.

"I don't think that's a good idea, she was a friend of her old family!"

I heard my uncle say, followed by a big slap on the desk. I jumped back, and knocked softly.

"Yes sweetie"

My dad said, completely changing his tone.

"I-I-I'm just trying to tell you I'm leaving soon, going on a date with Antonio. It's our first one."

Hoping he didn't get irritated with me, he came out the door and let out a huge gasp.

"You look beautiful. Baby remember what I told you, you don't have to do anything you don't want to or don't think you're ready for, what you do to night can determine how the rest of your life goes. I trust this Antonio kid, and I trust you, I want you to have fun, but not too much fun, okay?"

I shook my head, and he kissed me on the forehead. Before he shut the door I said

"I'm wearing moms necklace"

His head snapped back as if I said I killed somebody. I stepped back when I saw the anger, but a hint of sadness in his eyes.

"I'll take it off dad, I-I'm sorry." He lifted his arms, and I stepped further into the door.

"Baby, I'm not going to hurt you."

He was always bad with his rage, but even worse when he felt remorse...

"I'm going to go daddy."

I said still on defense, He just went into his room and shut the door. I felt a tear welling up but I knew I was about to have a good time, so I just ignored it.

I heard a honk outside so I grabbed my purse and phone then ran outside. I got in the front seat, and Antonio looked even happier than before.

"Babe, where are we going to eat?"

I could see him blushing, even though it was kind of dark outside.

"My parent's house."

My eyes popped open.

"Your parents! Babe why didn't you tell me! I'm so nervous. Wait your dad's name is Kareem right? Your mom and sister are Janae and April? Am I saying everything right?"

Antonio had a sparkle in his eye.

"I have a feeling we're going to go far, you'll do fine with my parents and little sister, you're amazing."

After a long ride we pulled up to this huge house, it even had gnomes, a pair of swans and sprinklers with flashing LED lights in the front yard.

"Wow, babe... I-I'm speechless." I said in awe.

"My parents opened an interior design center together, this was their first house, and look how they did together. It made their careers take off."

He said while he guided me down the walkway. The door was open, the house looked even better inside than the outside. There were two separate front rooms with 3 gold couches in one, 1 wrap around white couch in the other, with opposite color marble floors in each. It seemed as though the rooms were themed, they had certain family trip photos up, like the trip snowboarding in the room with the white couches, the trip to a place in Germany and Paris in the room with the gold couches. They even had a separate, smaller room with a love seat and a few colorful memory foam chairs with pictures from the wax museum in California. It was amazing, and I only just walked in.

"Where is everyone?"

I said, still looking around, I smelled something cooking in the pot, a strong scent of lasagna and greens. There was a fading scent of pie and cookies, probably being drowned by all the delicious food and seasonings. I smelt a hint of candy and butterscotch, it brought be back to the first time Antonio and I spoke, and it brought a huge smile to my face.

"My mom texted me, she ran to the store to grab some drinks, and some other things."

I shook my head,

"Where's your room baby?"

When I turned to look at him, he was already sweeping me off my feet and taking my up his white with gold polka dot spiral stair case.

"Don't drop me."

I said tightly wrapping my arms around his body.

"Relax"

He said with an assuring tone. He put me down when he got to the large black door, he stopped and put me down

"Open it."

He said, holding my waist. I was a bit spectacle, but when I opened the door there were white rose petals, butterscotch candles, a giant bear, and a big yellow pillow with my initials.

"What is this?"

I honestly didn't understand why he was doing all of this for me. "Baby, the first time I saw you was September 12th, when we started dating in October, the 12th was the day that we actually kissed for the first time, we were both so nervous that all we did was peck, or kiss each other on the cheek. The night of the 12ᵗʰ was also the day I told you about my life, and the first time you opened up to me about how you felt about me. I decided I would make the 12ᵗʰ a special day every month. This might be too soon, but I've never felt like this before. I think about you all day, Every time I see you my heart beats rapidly, I could listen to you talk all day. I love the way you talk, walk, think, smile, laugh, everything you can think of. I even like it when you're annoying me. I think, for the first time I might love somebody. I'm just glad it's you."

My heart felt like it dropped down to my stomach, I was speechless. He "loved" me... Me? He'd told me he never felt a spark with anybody, what did I do to make him feel this way about me? Whatever it was, I'm glad I did it, because for my first shot at dating, it was going pretty well. He held me like a baby, stared up to the wall while we were laying there. I could hear his heart beating... It almost put me to sleep.

We laid there in silence, until we heard the door open. Here they are. I thought to myself. When we got to the bottom of the stairs, Antonio's dad just gasped.

"She's beautiful son."

He said with a huge smile, and nod of approval. I said thank you, and hello to everyone else, I just hoped I didn't sound as nervous as I was. His little sister April was the cutest little girl I think I've ever seen. She had two long brunette pig tails with Red ribbons on each. She had on a black leotard and a red skirt with sparkly black flats. She was perfect, she ran right up to me when her father put her down. It was such a relief because I did not have a good track record when it came to children.

"You're pretty."

She said with her soft but high toned voice.

"Are you big brothers friend?"

She had the widest eyes and grin on her face.

"Well yes I am, and I've heard a lot about you."

She smiled and hoped out of my arms then grabbed my hand.

"Come eat with us."

she said as she pulled me in the direction of the kitchen. Antonio's mother just kept staring at me. At the dinner table, Antonio stood up and cleared his throat.

"This is my girlfriend, Kori Tucker, I've been knowing her for a little while now and I really like her, so get used to seeing her around."

I blushed and looked down at the folded napkin on my lap.

"You remind me of myself when I was younger."

Which were the words I hoped I'd hear when his mother spoke for the first time, after dinner, we had a chocolate chip pie, I never had one before but it was pretty good. Before we left I heard his little sister singing.

"I'm a little tea cup short and stout…"

I used to love this song when I was little.

"Here is my handle, here is my sprout."

I hummed aloud to myself.

"You're such a kid at heart."

Antonio said as he opened the door for me. I just could not get the song out of my head the whole night. The drive in was fun, I didn't get home until around 11 45 which was good because my curfew was at 12. I was so tired that as soon as I laid my head down I fell asleep.

I woke up after I had a strange dream. I was a little girl with a mom and dad, I had never seen those people before. I was in the middle of singing "I'm a little tea cup." It was raining so hard, we sped off the road. I couldn't hear anything, all I could feel was wind and the heavy rain drops hitting my face. Then I felt a sudden tug on my arm, as soon as I looked up there was a black shadow. I couldn't make the face out in time before I woke up, it was so creepy. I just stayed awake the rest of the night, ended up doing homework I wouldn't have done until Sunday. I got up later that morning when everybody else was actually awake, my dad was making omelets.

"Good morning"

I said, hoping he was in a better mood from yesterday.

"Good morning love, I'm making an apology breakfast."

Great. I said to myself, he still remembers. I noticed that he had a picture of my mother sitting on the counter. I still had her necklace on, we both must have been thinking about her.

"What do you have to do today?"

I said, breaking the silence.

"Nothing much, just going to run some errands with Aaron."

I could tell there was something wrong.

"Do you have something to tell me?"

I said with a concerned voice, walking towards him.

"I have somebody I wanted you to meet. Her name is Angela Pratt, we've been seeing each other for a while, so I think it's time."

I thought back to my dad and Uncle Sandy's argument, she must be the girl they were arguing about.

"Ok dad, I'll be happy to meet her."

I was hesitant to tell my dad about my dream but I couldn't get it out of my head, so I decided to wait until we were eating.

"Dad, I had a really weird dream last night, I was like 5 years old and I had different parents, it was raining really hard and we got into a car accident, after, I saw a figure grab me, but I couldn't make it out. I was singing I'm a little tea cup, I can't get the song out of my head."

His face looked like it was turning blue, as if he got sick. He stuttered hard,

"W-when did y-y-you, um…start thinking a-about this?"

He finally got the words out.

"Are you ok?"

I didn't understand why he got so creeped out about this dream.

"I'm fine baby, it's just a little weird. What else do you remember?"

He looked nervous and concerned

"I don't know pops, I think I'm just going to go back to sleep, I stayed up all night."

I said clearing my plate.

"Okay, I'll bring you some food home. See you later."

He didn't even look up at me. I wonder what that was about, I thought aloud. Kylah or Antonio hadn't responded to me yet, so I dozed off after an episode of my favorite cooking show, "Who's got next". My next dream was of me and Antonio on the beach, dancing and laughing. I was so glad I didn't have another bad dream, but every time I thought I got the song out of my head, it came right back. I spent my day worried about my dad, he just looked so stressed lately. He always told me he didn't tell me stuff because he didn't want to worry me, but I think that just made matters worse. My dad and I got along for the most part, but his anger used to get bad, his track record wasn't too good, and I don't really know much about him when I think about it. To me, he's always in his own world. No matter if he's with me, Uncle Sandy, at work, especially when he had nothing to do. I'm going to thinking about this for a while, I can tell. I should talk to my uncle Sandy about it, but I need to do a little digging about him too, maybe I'll find something in our extra room, some old pictures, yearbooks, love letters, something that'll lift the mystery in this house.

CHAPTER 3

I was greatly anticipating actually digging through things in the house. I felt like it was a violation, but I also feel a strain in between my father and I that I just can't shake. So, I decided to wait a little bit and chill out. I wanted to talk to Kylah, but I think it was a bit too personal, and could be confusing for her. I was laid out in bed, watching tv when my uncle walked in.

"Hey K crazy"

He said with what seemed like an excited tone, but I was not in the mood.

"Hey"

I said, pulling the covers over my body,

"I was just about to go to bed."

I hated lying to him, but I know if I told him what was on my mind he would tell me to

"Stay in a child's place"

just like my dad had always said. Uncle Sandy shrugged his shoulders and closed my door. A few minutes later I heard a car door shut, I looked out the window and it was Antonio. It was about weird seeing him now that I know how he really feels about me, so before he came in I hopped back in bed and pretended I was sleep. It didn't do much, a few moments later I heard the door creek open.

"Babe."

Antonio said, whispering like he wasn't trying to wake me up.

"I have chocolate chip pancakes."

I rolled over with a smile,

"You trying to make me fat so you can bake me aren't you?"

He laughed and walked over to sit on the edge of my bed.

"Why are you sleep?"

I rolled my eyes and looked at my phone.

"Um, it's Saturday, what else am I supposed to do?"

He had a muffled response because he decided to start stuffing his face. He put the fork that was piled with pieces of pancakes up to my lips,

"I'm not all that hungry love."

He looked disappointed

"But they're your favorite. What's wrong?"

I didn't want to talk, I just wanted to lay there alone, but I knew I couldn't shut him out because it wasn't his fault.

"I'll eat them later. I promise"

I said sticking my pinky out.

"Okay, it's a deal, I've got to go to practice so I'll see you later."

He leaned down and kissed my forehead. Before he left he turned and said

"Hey I like your sweats, where'd you get them from?"

We shared a laugh, he was so corny, one of the reasons I liked him. Maybe a half hour later my uncle Sandy said he was leaving for a few hours. So I was going to be home alone, again, with the haunting thoughts of whether or not I should go through some things in our extra room. So I decided to suck it up and go in there.

The first box I looked through were my baby pictures, I never really noticed that none of them were really close up. I was either on a park bench, through a glass in my hip hop dance class, playing in the park or leaving out my favorite ice cream shop. I saw a few pictures of my mother, she was so beautiful. She had the prettiest pregnancy glow. I just feel so bad that I was the one who killed her... Why did I have to be such a difficult birth? I always imagined that my mother and I would be the best of friends, and that maybe my dad wouldn't of drank so much... Gotten angry so often, maybe he could've been nice all around instead of feeling remorse after the fact. Maybe my dad and uncle Sandy wouldn't be so secretive, always arguing behind closed doors. I sighed after I got to the bottom of the box. I was about to give up until something caught my eye. It was my mothers' death certificate, signed November 12th, 1990.

"Overdose? Drowned?"

I felt the tears welling up in my eyes. I heard the front door open so I put everything back, except for the death certificate, I quickly folded it up and was on my way back to my room when my dad saw me.

"What are you doing?"

He said, raising his voice.

"Oh nothing, just going back to my room."

I said shaking, I could feel the paper falling from my shirt. "So why are you running."

I let out a sigh of relief, I thought he saw me coming out from the extra room.

"I don't want to miss the battle between the chefs, the commercials are about to end."

I said sneaking past him, I slipped into my room and fell on my bed.

"Murdered?"

I just couldn't believe my eyes. What else was hidden from me? Should I keep this to myself? I'm so confused, I'm hurt... I don't know what to do. I got up and rolled the certificate small enough to fit inside a coin holder, perfect hiding place I thought to myself. I climbed back into bed and closed my eyes,

"I'll just sleep on it."

I said a loud...

"I don't think it'll help though."

As soon as I let myself drift off into sleep I had the dream again. I still couldn't make out the face, but this time it was a little different. I was cold, and then I felt a sudden rush of heat, like I got back into a car or something. I saw a burst of flames and I jerked out of my sleep. I didn't know what was going on with me.

For a while after I woke up, I hadn't even thought about what I found, until I saw my dad and got a chill. Should I be afraid of him now? Why would he say my mom died at child birth, why was he so shaken up about my dream? I knew I had to act normal because I am meeting his new girlfriend later, I also didn't want him to put two and two together. It was around 5:00 and my dad had asked me to cook dinner. I rolled out of bed and down to the kitchen. I took out chicken earlier in the day, so I put that on the stove, along with macaroni and greens. I started the batter for the corn bread when my dad appeared in the doorway.

"She'll be here in about an hour."

I ignored him and continued to prepare the meal. I wasn't all that excited to meet her. I didn't want to jump to any conclusions but I was somewhat worried about her. Angela... such an innocent name. I started making up her life story simply for entertainment. She was the only child, graduated Blufordwith a 3.2 GPA then went on to Harvard on a full scholarship, graduated top of her criminal justice class... Actually no, Angela seem more like a pediatrician or something, she graduated at the top of that class. She was going to be married but it didn't end well, thank God she didn't get pregnant, maybe she did, that would be a good twist.

"A step brother or sister. Hmm."

I said, scratching my head wondering what it would be like to have a sibling. She better not be the evil step mother I used to think about when my dad dated other girls. Next thing you know; my uncle Sandy is going to be engaged to be married. I gave myself a headache day dreaming. It did take some of the boredom of cooking alone away.

My dad was probably upstairs putting on his best suit, along with his best jewelry. I hope she knows about his temper, and tendency to keep secrets. About an hour went by and I was setting the table, I remember getting my hands beaten with a ruler when I put the salad fork on the wrong side. I hated doing it, it always brought me back to that day my knuckles bled so bad I had to put three gauzes around them. I couldn't hold anything for like a week. My dad finally came downstairs in a nice button up, his favorite gold chain and some slacks. He me up the stairs to go change before the love of his life swooped in to take a permanent seat. Maybe I was being dramatic, but it made me sick having to know that he has been lying about my mother's death. I blamed myself all my life and he let me. I just couldn't believe it.

I slipped into my white dress that had colorful flowers on it. I liked it because it wrapped around my stomach but flowed at the bottom. I put my hair in a bun with my gold head band with the bow on the side and made my way downstairs. I don't see why I have to get dressed up in my house. The doorbell rang and my dad practically ran like he was on fire right to the door, then tried to act like he was calm right before he opened it. He was such a kid when it came to females. She walked in and my jaw dropped. She was beautiful. She was white and had long brunette hair that was perfectly wrapped into a bun, she had on a tight blue dress that had lace connecting the top of her back, she accessorized with silver jewelry and a nice pair of black heels. My dad introduced us, I went in for a hand shake but she went in for a hug. The first thing out her mouth was,

"I see we have the same taste in hair."

I smiled, I was just glad she wasn't evil like I had anticipated.

We sat down to eat and had normal enough conversation. I was right about a few things, she was the only child and she did go to Harvard. I also got a few things wrong, she graduated high school from my very own Chasity high, got her PhD in communication and bachelors in early childhood education. It seemed like my dad picked her right out of a "Perfect girlfriend" catalog. After dinner was over my dad joined her out for a night at the club, so once again I was home alone. I was expecting to see my uncle stroll through the door but that didn't happen. Antonio called me but I decided to ignore it. As soon as I saw my dad and Angela pull off, I went to grab my mother's death certificate. I skipped down to the "cause of death" section. I had to read it again. She drowned after falling asleep in the bathtub... she overdosed. I read the line over and over again.

"That doesn't make any sense!"

I said throwing the paper across the room. I couldn't breathe, I was angry and hurt at the same time. I threw my glass across the room and watched the shattered pieces fall to the floor, I knocked everything off of my nightstand. I unsuccessfully punched the wall, and when my knuckle began to bleed I put my back to the wall and let myself slide down it. Tears rolling down my face, I slapped them off my cheek. I was too angry to cry. I knew I had to find out the truth about my mother. I was just so scared to see something that I didn't want to. All I can hear is my dad's voice saying

"If you're looking for something you will find it, but it might not make anything better, and could make everything worse."

It made me angry because he was right! Do I want to uncover the truth? If I do what would I even do with that information besides keep it to myself. In fear of getting beaten, hidden away at another private school, or cut off from life itself. What if it's something much deeper than I'm letting myself think? I know my imagination is going to destroy me before the truth does. Unless both are as horrific as I think I finally know enough to bring it up to Kylah, hopefully I don't scare her away...

Sunday was a bleak day, and I was so excited to go to school and get out of this now unfamiliar house. I got all dressed up, I had on my black skirt, avengers half shirt, yellow cardigan and my favorite pair of black flats with sparkles, of course I topped it off with curly hair a bow and long dangling earrings. Antonio looked flawless. He took my breath away when I saw him, he had on an all-black outfit, one shiny gold earring, gold watch, two gold chains and of course his championship ring. When he saw me he picked me up and swung me around.

"Somebody's happy to see me."

I said holding him tightly. He would not stop kissing me, I could feel my cheeks burning with redness, I could only imagine how many people were staring at us. Then, to ruin the moment, Haley price came down the hall and grabbed his arm

"You disgust me!"

She said snapping at him, he put me down and pushed her away,

"Get off me yo"

He said wiping his shirt off. I stepped around him

"Is there a problem?"

she got closer to me

"yeah there is."

I laughed in her face

"Do something!"

I swiftly put my hair in a ponytail, everybody was crowded around us now, she jumped at me like I was supposed to shake, I put my arm back to swing, when all of a sudden I was being lifted off my feet and dragged away. I could hear her talking even when I was down the hall way.

"Put me down!"

I kicked and tried to break myself loose. A few moments later Antonio put me down

"Baby, she's not worth it."

I couldn't get the situation off my mind all day, I couldn't let it show though, I can't give her the satisfaction. Antonio walked off to go talk to his friend but I kept walking. A few moments later I managed to shake off the situation, I walked past the back door and I saw Kylah come in to school late, I was having second thoughts about telling her what was really going on… I just decided to tell her about my dad's new girlfriend. I start telling her about how horribly perfect she was, but she cut me off right after I finished describing her.

"What's her name?"

she said moving closer to me.

"Angela Pratt."

She gasped and looked like she saw a ghost. She screamed out "Ewe." loudly enough for the teacher to yell at us for not doing our group work.

"That's my mom!"

She said before I could fix my mouth to ask her what's wrong.

"Bu-bu-but your last name is Jackson!"

I said with an expression of disbelief stuck on my face.

"Jackson is my dad's last name!"

I couldn't believe what I was hearing, when my dad dropped me off at Kylah's house all those times before he never cared to mention that this oddly perfect girlfriend of his was my best friend's mother! I had to process a few things before I could even respond. I don't understand why he wouldn't just tell me. It's not like it's that big of deal, I wouldn't mind if I could officially call Kylah my sister. I decided not to text him about it, instead just wait until I got home. I'm going to try to keep on topic, I'm just so afraid that the thing about my mom's death certificate would spew out. I was still so angry about that. We had a substitute in English so Kylah and I decided to skip it.

Walking through the hallways I saw my friend Jacob, I knew he had the biggest crush on me so I tried to avoid him for the most part, but he didn't have anywhere to be.

"Hey beautiful"

He said grabbing my hand. He and Kylah had a love hate relationship, she smacked his hand down off me and said

"Back off perv she has a boyfriend."

Oddly enough Antonio was walking down the hall way.

"Yeah and that boyfriend is me! Back off boy."

He said walking at a quick speed to get over there. Jacob backed up, if only I didn't have to work with him in a group, I thought to myself.

"babe he was kidding relax."

A teacher stuck his head out his door and yelled at us to get to class, thankfully at the right time, I was certainly in no position to tell Antonio to keep his cool.

"Yo baby I need you to start knocking dudes out."

He said boxing the air.

"Whatever Mr. Tough guy"

I said sarcastically

"who you looking so good for today?"

Antonio always acts so modest when it comes to his looks because he doesn't want to act like the

"Typical high school athlete/ average boy next door"

in his words anyway, but he always sucked it up for me, or I would go on and on about him until he cracked.

"You of course babe."

He said grabbing my hands.

"today has been way to eventful for it to still be morning."

The bell had already rung for homeroom, but nobody around here really cared, so around the shop area there were students coming from every direction. I already knew we had a substitute so I wasn't in a rush. Kylah and I decided to walk Antonio to class, he had History with Mr. Garvin, he was a strange man, but everybody I knew liked him, I wouldn't be seeing him for another year so I wasn't too worried about it. After Antonio and I kissed goodbye Kylah said she wanted to go to her friend Tyler's classroom so she could get a charger. I decided to take advantage of this time and tell her what I've been wanting to get off of my chest.

"So since your mom is dating my dad I feel like I should tell you what he's really like."

Kylah looked shocked because I always brush her off when she asks why I never really talk about him, and why I always talk about my uncle.

She was also concerned about me retelling the same 4 stories and repeating

"We're as thick as thieves."

I knew she was getting tired of the run around.

"I never wanted to really talk about him because I didn't always enjoy his company. When I was turning 8 he started drinking a lot, when I say a lot, I mean he had me running to get his bottles, my uncle Sandy and my dad almost got into a fight over it. I have no idea why he was so angry. I always figured he was grieving my mother...But I never understood why he began to get violent after two years of being an alcoholic. One day he was telling me that I looked just like her, He was taking a big gulp of his vodka in between almost every word. He was sweating, and couldn't stand up straight, I remember him snapping his head to the side and whispering something to himself. I couldn't make it out, but I was too scared to ask him what was going on. I was only 12, so I got out of bed and asked him if he wanted help getting to the bed. I tried to grab the bottle, and that was the first time he struck me."

I took a pause before I was going to begin my sentence again.

"I don't know if I want to hear this."

I could understand her concern but I just felt like it was her responsibility not only because she's my best friend but because she needs to know what type of man her mom is getting involved with. I just ignored the comment and kept talking.

"It was a quick blow to the face, I stumbled back into my bed and started screaming. He was stumbling towards me and I thought that he was going to hit me over the head with his bottle. But instead he grabbed my hair, sweat dripped off his face, it was no longer plastered with the expression of anger, but it was replaced with despair... All in an odd swift motion he dropped his bottle and fell to his knees. I joined him, I slowly moved to embrace him. After a while of intense silence, my uncle finally came in to find him. He always seemed to save me, this time he was a bit too late, he cleaned me up and apologized for my father, I understood him not staying to console me because he would have been preoccupied... So I just cried alone... My father, so overcome with sadness, my mother, dead... That night, was the first time I had ever took her picture out of my drawer and really looked at it. I had blamed myself all those years because if she hadn't of had me, she would've been alive."

We got to Tyler's classroom so I put my story on hold. Kylah was being unusually silent. I figured it was because all those times she had asked me to share, she never expected that to come out of my mouth, when she finally did say something, it was exactly what I expected.

"I had no idea things were like that, when I asked I definitely thought it would be something like, he was never around or he used to punish you, I'm so sorry for prying."

I just wanted to really get the root of the conversation out of the way before we went to our separate classes until English 9th period.

"When I went to Antonio's house, his little sister April was singing I'm a little tea cup. I couldn't get it out of my head. That night when I went to sleep I had a dream about my child self in a car accident. A shadow appeared next to me, but I couldn't make it out. It took me from the car and I watched it explode. When I told my dad about it, he was so shaken up and began to act so weird, he left in a hurry too. There's an extra room in our house that we use solely for junk, I started looking through a bin with lots of papers and photos in it, and I came across my mother's death certificate. It said that she died from drowning. I can't see how that would make sense so I've been wrecking my brain about it for days."

Kylah looked like she was really trying to give me an answer, I didn't expect much but I appreciated her trying. The bell rung and we walked away, both worried and thinking about the same thing. I didn't see Antonio like I usually do when I walk up the stairs near the cafeteria, but I just carried on to class. I pretty much slept in every one up until English, I knew that would be a busy class. Kylah and I didn't really speak much to each other, but we were partners in the project we got assigned. It was called "Pick your tragedy." It was 60% of our grade, but it was very interesting.

We were to search online for tragedy's that happened anywhere our state or city. We were to write what happened including all the facts of the tragedy, when, where, who and how many people were involved, but there was a twist. After we did the research part of the paper, we were supposed to make our own version of the story, no matter how dark, different, or twisted it was. We had to say why we thought that, and had to make sure we connected everything with the actual evidence, we only had two weeks to do it. I was so excited for this because I loved creative writing. Kylah was excited because she wants to diagnose somebody. She wanted to be a Clinical psychologist so bad, I admired her for knowing what she wanted to do so early in the year. She gave us time to get everything organized and start to look stuff up, we didn't find anything that quickly though. We decided to meet at the library around 5 o'clock, I was looking forward to time away from the house. The time flew for the rest of the day and I was headed home to talk to my father about why he neglected to tell me his girlfriend was my best friend's mother. I had Antonio drop me off before he went to practice and I burst into the door.

"What is wrong with you! You just scared me!"

My dad yelled, so I yelled back

"Why didn't you tell me your girlfriend was Kylah's mom! As soon as you dropped me off to her mom's house the first time you should've told me!"

He just shook his head

"I was going to tell you; it must've just slipped my mind."

I rolled my eyes.

"I'm going to the library at 5."

He jumped at the opportunity to make things better.

"I'll take you."

By that time, I was so annoyed I just told him I would walk and stomped up to my room. Along with my other homework I decided to bring the death certificate, maybe we could come to a conclusion about that. I changed into sweats and walked out the door without saying bye, I could feel myself losing love and gaining suspicion, I never thought I would feel like this towards him. I have forgiven him for a lot of things but if there is something that's been going on my whole life that I deserved to know, I don't think I ever could forgive, love or trust him again.

CHAPTER 4

By the time I got to the library, Kylah was already waiting for me with two pieces of pizza and soda for each of us.

"Ugh, where have you been all my life!"

I said swinging my book bag on to the chair. Kylah laughed, but then went back to her serious face.

"What happened with your dad?"

I had just begun to get that off my mind, but as soon as she said it I got furious all over again.

"I don't know, I just can't think straight right now, everything that's been going on is all so…weird, but I'm trying not to jump to conclusions."

Kylah just nodded her head. I sighed and began to remove my books from my bag and lay them out on the table.

"So first we need to figure out what kind of tragedy we're looking for."

Kylah popped up and said

"I have an idea!"

It really looked as if she had a lightbulb and party streamers coming out of her head.

"Why don't we look up a family that died in a car accident, see if there is anything like it that you could remember."

I would not have thought of that. It seems like it's the universes way of telling me I should find the truth or at least see if I'm crazy or not. Kylah pulled out her laptop as I got my notebooks out, ready to write. We went through a few tragedies in minutes, it was surprising how many accidents kill so many people.

"*6 people killed in an untimely collision.*"

"*Teen, pregnant with twins, killed by a drunk driver.*"

"*Coach bus with 18 kids, hit by a metro bus, pushed over a bridge.*"

They were all tragedies, but none of them related to what we wanted, right when we were going to take a break, we saw it." *Family of 3, killed in a car crash that blew up in flames.*" I couldn't believe it, what if this was what I've been dreaming about. The neighborhood seemed so familiar to me. "Court and Elm avenue." I said it out loud to try to process it better but it didn't work.

Full and ready to go, Kylah says

"You ready to get an A?"

I loved her enthusiasm. I remembered that I had my mother's death certificate. I pulled it out.

"Before we start, I need you to see something. Tell me I'm not crazy."

She looked it over, I could see her eyes pop open.

"It really says she drowned…Now I'm really in!"

She slammed her paper down and clicked the link to the news report. I began to make the draft sheet,

Family of 3, killed in a car crash that blew up in flames.

When: January 15, 1992

Where: Tampa Bay Florida

Why: Good question…What is our theory going to be…What do I think happens in my dreams? We have to think of something good.

Who: Chasity Powers, 34-year-oldhouse wife. Carson Powers, 37-year-old real estate agent and their 5-year-old daughter, Cassie Powers.

Kylah's poster changed, she leaned back in her seat and dropped her shoulders, I could tell that this project would get to her. In the news report it said that the Power family was greatly known in the community, they were perfect, right down to their picket fence. Chasity had always watched the neighborhood children when their parents were at work, she'd throw these amazing parties and volunteer at homeless and battered woman shelters, she was the modern Mother Theresa. Carson Powers was the best real estate agent in Florida, he supposedly sold the mayor 3 of his houses and owned a few himself. He made sure his business didn't go down by making sure the neighborhood stayed in tac. The daughter, Cassie Powers hadn't quite made her mark yet, the only thing it said was that she went to a private school and was the poster child for kinder-garden.

"This is truly a tragedy."

I said shaking my head. It wasn't just that they were an upper class family with the community at their feet, it was just the fact that bad things happen to good, bad, and indifferent people all the time. There was no specific karma for bad people vs good. This felt so personal, I think it's just because in the back of my head I wanted to make this connection to my dreams. It was getting dark, and there was a strange distanced in between Kylah and I, I was ready to call it a night. When we were putting everything away I couldn't stand the silence, and I couldn't let it go.

"Are you okay Kylah?"

I said concerned, she shrugged her shoulders

"I don't know it's just things like this really get to me, and I'm actually really worried about you. What if we end up uncovering something that changes your life? What if something bad happens in the process of doing this? I know you hate when I over think but these pros and cons need to be laid out."

I knew what she meant, I was scared too, I weighed those options and thought about backing out, I knew I couldn't.

"You don't have to help me as long as you're still there for me. Like I've said before, I know that my imagination is going to rip me to shreds at night and all day. I won't be able to handle not knowing. I don't want to make you feel obligated and definitely not uncomfortable."

I just really wanted her to make sure this didn't put a strain on our relationship and didn't change her clear and sweet perception on life. Kylah had a good life, and I admire her for being optimistic, nothing had ever broken her heart or traumatized her, she was just a bundle of joy. I loved her, I couldn't be the one to tint her sense of life.

"I'll just think about it. We can meet up tomorrow at my place or yours to keep working on the project."

Kylah said grabbing her bag and hopping out the chair.

"We'll figure it out."

I said collecting my thinks and following her out the door. I seriously dreaded having to go home, I did not want to deal with the blow back of my explosion earlier today. To my surprise the house was empty when I returned, so I showered and got into bed. I called Antonio but he didn't answer. I wondered what he was doing but I didn't want to make a big deal out of anything. I didn't have any homework to do, and I really didn't feel like getting up to pick out my outfit for school so I just continued to be bored. About an hour went by and my dad came in with Angela, it felt so strange knowing that she's Kylah's mom. I just ignored the fact that they came in and got up to turn up my music. On my way to the speaker, I heard them pop a bottle, my dad hasn't had a drink for almost a year now, half of me was happy that Angela may see the real side of him, and the other half was worried it may turn out bad for both of us. I decided to call Antonio again, I was so glad he answered.

"What's up baby? I'm just leaving practice."

I took a glance at the clock, it was 9, I wasn't going to speak on his late practice because he very well may have been practicing at this time of night considering how serious he is about his sports.

"I want to get out of this house, help me?"

I said trying to sound as desperate as possible. It took a while but he finally responded.

"Yeah babe I'll come get you but I'm with some friends."

I hurried to grab some clothes to put on and look half way presentable.

"Did you want to go somewhere in specific?"

He said, still telling his friends to quiet down.

"No baby I'll go wherever you were planning on going."

"Alright I'm on my way, be ready."

After he said that I heard a bunch of his friends making jokes, saying he was "whipped" and a "cub", he hung up before I could hear anything else. I threw on my ripped high waist jeans a black half shirt and a long white cardigan with my black timberlands. I threw my hair in a bun, grabbed my hoop earring and a purse and headed down the stairs. I was trying to walk out without speaking but of course my dad said something.

"Where ae you going?"

He said, catching his breath from his roaring laughter. I'm sure whatever she said wasn't that funny.

"Antonio is outside we're going to go to the movies."

He put his glass down and came closer to me,

"You weren't going to say bye?"

he grabbed my arm, part of me wanted to make a scene so Angela could see how he is, but before I said anything she was telling my dad to relax.

"It's fine, just let her go, she probably just didn't want to interrupt."

He looked at her in shock and I snatched my arm back,

"Yeah, I just didn't want to interrupt."

I flew out the door before he could respond. I'm so glad Angela stepped in. I ran to Antonio's car and rolled my eyes when I realized I had to sit in the back, at least it was James and Chris, the two of his best friends I could actually stand.

"I'm sorry babe, I'm dropping them off soon, we just have to make a few stops first."

He leaned back and kissed me. Of course his friends made a huge production out of it, it was so embarrassing. I stayed in the car when they went into the sporting goods store, and the dollar store. They were throwing their annual "Athlete only" party, which I heard gets crazier every year. I was a bit worried because the cheerleaders, volleyball players, soccer players, and every other sport with drop dead gorgeous females with to die for bodies are going to be there. I can't show my insecurities and just trust the fact that Antonio loves me...I at least hope that's the case. I'm just secretly hoping that when the time comes, he'll invite me. Antonio and his two friends got back in the car

"Look what I got you babe."

Antonio held up a females' basketball jersey with his number "3" on it

"You can be my biggest fan now."

I couldn't make the comment I wanted to considering we weren't alone, but his friend James took care of that for me.

"Yo, her thirst traps about to be...!"

He said shaking his head and slapping up Chris. I blushed so hard and bust out laughing. I pushed his shoulder and told him to shut up! Antonio didn't get mad since he was one of his bestfriend's. He just laughed along. I wonder if he was tired of waiting... All we've ever done was kiss, we never even got close to sleeping together. There were no "thirst traps" or even a discussion about, now that I think about it, we're completely overlooking that part in our relationship. I'm really not sure if that was a good thing or not, I didn't know if I should bring it up either. After everybody was dropped off, Antonio pulled over to an empty parking lot and we just cuddled in the back seat. I was curious to know whether or not he was just content on not sleeping with me or getting something from somebody else.

"So... Are we ever going to talk about...taking that next step?"

I dreaded the moments it took for him to respond.

33

"I don't want to rush you into anything. I know you're a virgin, I want to make sure this is a decision you want to make with me."

I had never really told him I was a virgin, he just assumed. I knew he had been around with like, 13 different girls minimum... I could see why he would want me to make sure I was ready. I wouldn't know what I would do if I was just a notch on someone's belt. I honestly didn't feel like that would be the case with him.

"Do you love me?"

It was so tense in the car I could feel my body heating up.

"I do."

Antonio said clutching my hand even tighter than before.

"I'm ready."

He looked me in my eyes for what seemed like hours. He traced my face with the slightest touch of his fingertips. I grabbed his hand and slipped my fingers in between his. I anticipated a kiss, a spark and then some romantic background music. Instead of a kiss on the lips I got a kiss on the cheek.

"I want I to be special, not in my car or planned. I love you."

I looked up at him, looking down on me... I shook my head and we just laid there for about a half hour longer until he took me home. I went straight up to my room after I saw Angela's shoes still near the door. I called Kylah

"I see your parentless for the night."

"Yeah, my mom called and said she wouldn't be coming home. I could be doing something bad right now and she wouldn't even know."

"My dad hasn't called at all and its pushing 12am, I know he didn't hear me come in because that old folk's music is blasting."

"Apparently we're trust worthy." We both shared a laugh.

"So... Me and Antonio finally-..." She cut me off

"Please spare me the details, actually, don't!" She was so disgusting it was hilarious.

"We didn't actually do it, we just talked about it for the first time. I thought it was going to happen after I told him I was ready, but instead he just kissed me cheek and said he wanted it to be special."

Now that I'm saying it out loud it does kind of seem strange but sweet at the same time. I couldn't get it out of my head actually... I continued on to say

"I really wonder how it will be, will it hurt? Would it be weird after?

What if I don't know what to do. I'm more nervous thinking about it now. I wish we would've did it, now I'm just stuck with my imagination once again."

"Maybe he really does want it to be special or maybe he's getting something from someone else."

I was very surprised at her brutal honesty.

"Ugh, don't say that!"

I said shaking my head.

"I would be so hurt I would never come back to school or ever come over to your house again!"

She made the dramatic theme music, I hated when she was being sarcastic. We talked for a few more minutes until she finally said she was going to go to bed. The events of the day were so irritating. I was ready for it to be over but I couldn't fall asleep. I watched the clock go from 12 to 1 to 2, then I just stopped watching the clock. I got up, got in the shower, listened to every song on my playlist, played against myself in scrabble, got a mat and exercised and I still wasn't tired. By then it was almost time for me to get up for school anyways, so I just took time out to curl my hair and pin it up. Around 6 I heard my dad and Angela laughing, there was a slight smell of coffee and bagels, so I took it they didn't make enough for three. I got my usual good morning text from Antonio, since I was pretty much ready I told him he could pick me up before his meeting so we could grab breakfast. I would have to suck it up and sit on the bleachers to wait for him. For the first time this year I had on sweats and sneakers. I knew everybody would think something was wrong considering I was always dressed in Sunday's best. I had to throw on a bunch of jewelry and put on mascara with eyeliner on to make up for my lack of effort towards my outfit. I slipped out the door unnoticed about 45 minutes later.

"Hey K."

Antonio said, I wasn't sure if it was too early or if it was a distance between us, but I just decided to ignore it. I gave him a kiss and sat back in my seat, it was a quiet ride to Breakfast Town, but still I ignored it. Antonio opened my door for me and held my hand, ordered, paid for our food and still barely talked to me, when we got into the car I had to speak up.

"Is there something wrong? Something that I should know about?"

All he did was shake his head. It couldn't have been anything I did, we were doing so well.

"How is everybody at home?"

I got a shoulder shrug again.

"Pull over!"

I said hitting his arm. He kept driving, so I got louder

"Pull over!"

I said, getting so angry my voice cracked. He pulled over to side of the road and rubbed his face.

"What's wrong? Talk to me!"

I had to put my nice comforting voice back on because by then I was actually worried.

"You know last night I would've loved to take care of you... I would've loved to kiss up and down the length of your body, I would've loved to be your first... Yesterday I was prepared to make you fall deep inlove with every move I made."

I was so confused.

"So what stopped you?"

He shook his head like he didn't believe I was asking him that question.

"You know you haven't told me you loved me not one time? I put my heart on my sleeve when I brought you to my parent's house, I tell you when we get off the phone, when I drop you off, I told you last night and got the same response! A smile and a deep stare... If I'm wasting my time with you, you need to tell me right now. I won't be mad and we can still be friends."

I tried to think back to all the times he said it, I really didn't even know I hadn't said it, or that it's been bothering him for this long. I took off my seat belt and got closer to him, he still wasn't looking at me so I grabbed his face and tried to turn it but he wouldn't budge. I took a long deep breath.

"Baby, I'm so sorry, I do love you. I love you... I love you, I love you, I love you."

I said it as many times as I could remember he had, with a kiss on the cheek in between each.

"Do you forgive me?"

I said holding onto his hand. He shook his head and leaned over to give me a kiss. I was so relieved... I don't know what I would've done if he had left me.

"Let's just skip school today, nobody will be at my house all day."

I got excited

"Yes! I wasn't in the mood to go anyways."

He turned the car around and we headed back to his place. This was going to be the most relaxing day ever! I felt bad leaving Kylah to fend for herself in English but for sure she would understand. When we got to the house, of course Antonio carried me up the stairs. I could tell it would be our thing. After he laid me on the bed he started turn on his game and get comfortable. While I was eating cookies I saw on his desk, I took a glance to my side and saw a pink sweater hanging out of a box. I got up to grab it and it was an entire box of clothes, perfumes, earrings and shoes. I took advantage of the fact that Antonio was paying no attention to me. I quietly rummaged through the box and found a letter. It read

Dear Antonio,

You've been so good to me when I knew at times I didn't deserve it. I know you told me you tried to love me but couldn't, I just want you to try one more time. I hope you don't think me trying to end my life had anything to do with you, I've just been so confused. You know everything that has been going on with my family, my dad getting cancer, my mom's affair… I know I hurt you, or maybe I didn't, considering you never felt the way I did… Now that I think about it, I don't really know why I'm writing this letter other than I'm trying to make an ass out of myself. I have visiting hours now. Please call or come to see me… please.

Sincerely, Haley.

I could finally see why she was so angry, the letter had been balled up, he never responded to her and she was pouring her heart out. I put it back down and went over to bed. I was so bored watching him play the game so I decided to get his attention. I took off my sweats and threw them next to him, took off my shirt and did the same. He looked back to see me with my burgundy matching bra and panty set.

"You're perfect."

He said putting down his controller. He climbed onto the bed and pulled me on top of him.

"So you said you love me?"

He scanned my body like he was trying to study every inch of me. I shook my head in agreement.

"I need you to say it."

Now he was gripping the inside of my thighs. My heart was racing and my mind was blank. This was it, I was finally going to show my love... I just hoped I was right for this decision. I whispered

"I love you."

Slowly in his ear, it was up hill from then. It reminded me of a movie in slow motion, I played my own background music in my head, everything was perfect. I lasted an hour and 34 minutes exactly, I just happened to have glance at the time right before we actually went through with it. We laid there quiet and holding hands... We had lunch, then Antonio had desert... When I thought about him in that way before, I did him a disservice. While I was getting my things together I realized I needed to walk slowly. I thought people over exaggerated, but it was something serious. I felt like a grown woman, a brand new woman before anything. I couldn't stop grinning, and Antonio would not stop staring at me, and telling me he loved me. He admitted to me that he was nervous, I didn't understand because he had done it multiple times before... He had never made *love* before. He dropped me off at my house and of course nobody was there. I was happy because I had to erase the message my school sent saying that I was absent today. I had to get in the shower again, even though I didn't want to wash of the tingling feeling I had. Kylah happened to call me as soon as I got out.

"Guess what you missed today!"

she said before I got to say hello.

"Did the queen B come to our school?"

"No, horrible guess by the way. It was a fight!"

I was definitely surprised. Everybody in Chasity got along for the most part.

"Who fought?"

"Duke Redon and some boy named Josh, I heard they fought because Duke hit his girlfriend, I don't really know but I did see the fight. For Duke to be so big he sure did get beat up!"

We both laughed, I know Antonio won't let it go when he finds out.

"I have something to tell you."

I couldn't wait to tell her we actually did it, and that it was amazing.

"What, did you and Antonio finally seal the deal?"

"How did you know?"

"Why else would you skip school unless you were with him, and you were just talking about how you told him you were ready. How was it? Were there fireworks?"

"It was amazing, he made me feel so comfortable and so pretty. We laid together for like hours after. I really do love him."

"That's good, I hope you two last. Maybe soon Chase and I will be joining you in your conquest. But ok I have to go I got tons of homework which you have to make up!"

"Okay but where are we meeting up for the project, you could just do your homework with me."

"Oh yeah that's right. I'll be over soon I don't feel like being in this house anymore anyways."

We hung up the phone and I continued getting dressed. I had replays of me and Antonio over and over again. The way he rubbed my skin and picked me up so effortlessly, how he kissed and looked at me… I skipped around my room and listened to all love songs and waited for Kylah, she got here within the hour. When she said she had tons of homework she was not kidding. It felt like the one day I didn't come was the day out of the year that counted the most.

"Check the mailbox for your report card, they came out late but I got mine today. I only got an 86 average, but I did pass history!"

Kylah was smart, but some people just aren't "A" students. I ran down to the mailbox and grabbed my report card. A 95.32 average. I was used to it but I actually hardly applied myself this year. We began working on the project again. It was pretty straight forward and we already had the facts straight. One day, the Power's family went through their daily routine. Taking their daughter to school so they could go to work. It just happened to be fatal. "A slippery road." I don't know why that stuck with me so much, they said a slippery road was the reason for this Kodak family to start their day normally and end the rest of their days in flames. "I can't help but think about what type of morning they were having. Did they wake up and listen to jazz, dance around the house and laugh hysterically? Did the community have them all wrong? Was there violence and hurt in that house? I…I just can't help but want to know how it feels to not know your life is about to end."

I could not stop making up scenarios in my head.

"Are you sure you want to work on this project? We could choose like 100 bunnies dying from an oil spill or something."

I tried to pretend it was funny and giggled, but my heart felt like It was dropping into my stomach, each vessel snapping slowly… I didn't mean to be dramatic, but it didn't really feel like I was. I got a huge headache, we had to take a break for now.

CHAPTER 4

It was around 6 and my dad just came in and started cooking. He didn't even come up stairs to check on me. I guess he was still mad about last night.

"I can't help but get a little nervous when I know your dad is here... He was so nice when I met him I can't believe he did those things..."

I just shrugged my shoulders,

"before I was exposed to other people's lives I just thought it was normal... Sure I was unhappy but I just figured everybody was unhappy. I put on a smile every single day, doesn't every one?"

She began to reply when my door swung open and my uncle Sandy appeared.

"What's going on in this house! I'm gone for a couple of days and Martin is drinking again!"

Kylah started grabbing her things.

"No, stay"

I said, blocking her from picking up her last book.

"Uncle Sandy, can we talk outside please?"

She sat back down and we left the room.

"Look, I'm 17 years old and I cannot be held responsible for a grown man, if he wants to get drunk with his girlfriend I can't stop him!" I could see the rage in his eyes but I wasn't backing down, I would not be blame for my fathers' indiscretions. "You know he gets out of control, he could've hurt you! I wasn't here to stop him this time."

"I know…I left when I saw him drinking for that reason."

"So, you met his girlfriend… I didn't want him to introduce you two but I guess he didn't listen. I'll try to fix everything with Martin but no matter what you and your friend need to stay in your room unless I tell you otherwise."

I went back and closed the door. "What's going on? Are you ok?"

I know Kylah was worried but she just doesn't know the half… My dad's drunkenness never stopped with the beatings… Along with his hallucinations and arguments with himself there were night terrors… He woke up screaming and sweating, just to calm down and take another shot. He even got so drunk he passed out in the shower and hit his head, he was in the hospital for days… He set a bunch of photos on fire then attempted to put it out by supplying it with lighter fluid, thinking it was water. So of course that resulted in a half burned house and us having to relocate. I had flash back after flash back. I was probably sitting there with a blank face for a while. Kylah just sat there with me until we were both snapped back to reality after we heard glass smash on the ground.

"Just ignore it."

Kylah didn't listen to me, she ran over to the door to listen, I had enough of hearing the arguments between them so I just remained on the bed.

"Wow, this argument sounds so serious. I wonder what they're fighting about."

I could tell Kylah had that "you let my daughter eat ice cream when I said no" drama at her house, I wish I could say that… We heard three repeated slams on the wall that shook the whole house, that made me get up too. I opened the door an inch a minute so it wouldn't make any noise. I'm so happy we have carpet and not hardwood so I wouldn't have to attempt to levitate when Kylah and I went to the top of the steps. We saw my dad, drunk of course, hemmed up against the wall by my uncle Sandy… This couldn't just be because he was drinking again. Kylah grabbed my hand and squeezed it, I was somewhat used to this but she picked a horrible time to come. They were just standing looking at each other eye to eye for several moments until my uncle finally started talking.

"You took her so you could have the child you took away from yourself! I helped you be a father so you could get over your condition, not so you can get drunk and make her life hell! Especially not bring back crucial people from her past that could get us caught!"

Kylah got up and went back into the room in awe, but I was stuck. Was he talking about me? What did he mean when he said my dad had *"took"* me? I heard him say that he didn't want my dad to see Angela before, had I met her already? I was so confused I didn't hear my dad give a response but I saw my uncle let him go so I ran back to my room. Kylah and I sat there in silence until a few moments later my uncle came in and told me to spend the night at Kylah's house. It was silent when I was getting my clothes together and so was the ride over there. Now that I think about it my mind was blank, I wasn't over thinking or trying to make sense of any of the recent events. When we got to Kylah's house we were the only people there. We went straight up to her room without saying a word. I was laying my things out when I saw Kylah typing something up on her lap top.

"What are you doing?"

I said with no expression other than pure sadness in my voice.

"Well, we haven't looked at any pictures of the Powers family, let's see if there is a resemblance."

My heart was beating out of my chest, this was it, the moment I put two and two together, the moment where my life could change forever. A few moments later the photo popped up. It felt like my eyes were focusing just like a camera, trying so hard not to see the truth. I heard Kylah gasp.

"Oh my God, Kori!"

I bust out crying,

"Look at the picture Kori!"

Kylah just kept yelling but I couldn't. I pushed the laptop away and watched it hit the floor. I felt sick, her reaction was reassuring enough, I knew it was me... I knew I wasn't having that dream for no reason. I stumbled to the bathroom and Kylah followed, she kept badgering me

"You have to see the photo for yourself Kori, this is what you wanted!"

She grabbed my arm and I snatched it back and fell to my knees, I could barely get my words out.

"No... I wanted to be wrong! I wanted the secrecy and my mother's death to all just be a misunderstanding, I wanted the problem to be that we were going broke and that we were going to lose the house. I wanted to have a long lost sister or I hoped my dad or uncle lead a different life that didn't result in me being a freaking Janie doe!"

My eyes stung with each tear that dropped from it. My imagination could not have been this bad. My father is not my father. I was not myself. I had to puke, I was in the bathroom for almost an hour throwing up and trying to tell myself I was ok and to get up. I had no energy and I looked pale, my eyes were sunk in, face raw and eyes blood shot. I still looked better than I felt. I basically dragged myself back to Kylah's room, when I got there I saw her crying. My voice was still raspy and cracking

"What's wrong?"

She didn't even look up, since she was white she lit up like a stop light, her freckles even turned red.

"Remember when your uncle said that he shouldn't be bringing back people from your past? I decided to look into it... There was an interview with people who lived on the street and were known friends of the Power family..."

She turned the laptop to face me and my jaw dropped. The head line was "Angela Jackson, best friend of Chasity Powers, speaks on her feelings about the accident" I had no idea that would be the connection between us.

"Why didn't my mom recognize you? I knew it was strange that we had an immediate connection."

Kylah was still wiping tears from her face. We just laid there replaying the video over and over again.

"Do you want to look at the picture now?"

I took a deep breath and shook my head to give her the ok. I watched her click back on to the previous browser. When the picture popped back up it was exactly what I thought it was going to be. My parents looked like they were beautiful people. I heard a voice in my head, I couldn't make it out, it was so muffled, it was a woman's voice, could I have remembered my mother's voice? I could hear I'm a little tea cup playing over and over in my head. I knew it was something that clicked when I heard April singing that song. I must have fell asleep because I jerked myself out of a dream where I was a child again, living back with the parents I was taken from... Was I really taken from them? Part of me wanted to think that it was all a dream, but I knew it wasn't.

My uncle, the one person I trusted with my life is the one that helped my actual life get taken from me. Was it a coincidence that my parent's and I got in a car accident? If it was then how did my dad... Martin even come in contact with me? Was it all a plan? My head felt heavy with questions and I wasn't sure if I wanted to go to school or not, I didn't want to fall behind but I felt like I had more important work to do. Kylah was asleep next to me. It was 3 in the morning and so many questions were running through my mind. Would I be able to get the answer alone? I didn't want to drag Kylah through any more of this, today was the first time I've seen her show any emotion other than happiness and I didn't like it. I needed her bubbly attitude to get through this hard time but I knew she wouldn't let me go through this alone. I did end up making it back to sleep just to get up a few hours later.

When Kylah got up I made my decision to go to school, if I was going to get anything accomplished I had to make sure I acted as if nothing was wrong and I had to make sure all my snooping was timed right. It was just one question I could not shake…Who's death certificate did I find? I know that my uncle said that my dad "took" a child from himself. I don't know, I think I was letting everything cloud my judgement. I just pushed everything to the back of my mind and got dressed. Antonio called me but I let it go to voicemail, I hoped he just shook it off and didn't think anything serious. As soon as I got to school people were already being loud and obnoxious, I smiled and laughed along because what I was going through was nobody's fault. Around 5th period I was called down to the office for dismissal. I really didn't want to see my uncle and especially not my dad. To my surprise it was Angela. Why would she be picking me up instead of Kylah. My heart was racing, I hoped she didn't hear what me and Kylah were talking about, but she couldn't have because she wasn't home. I have to sit in her face for whatever reason and withhold the information that I have. I was hesitant walking towards her and I refused to make eye contact, I didn't ask her why she was picking me up and she didn't care to mention it. We drove about 25 minutes out of town to a random coffee shop, everything looked so suspect to me. I kept my mouth shut and just followed her in, still she didn't say a word. It was a total population of 5 people including us, so you could hear a pen drop. She sat down and ordered a triple cream triple sugar coffee and asked me if I wanted anything, I shook my head and scooted down in my seat. When the coffee came she cleared her throat.

"I remember you."

She said it so nonchalantly it concerned me.

"I don't know what you mean."

I said shrugging my shoulders, on the inside my stomach turned and I could feel my sweat rising on my skin. "I knew your mother."

"My mother is dead."

"I know she is. But your mother is not who you think she is, not who you've been told she is, anyways."

"I don't know what you mean." We went back and forth like it was a battle of who would break first.

"I think you do."

"Well I don't." She sipped her coffee and began to laugh.

"She was my best friend, I told her all my problems and she told me hers. We went to the movies and we went shopping, we got pregnant around the same time, delivered in the same week, we even had our baby shower together. You know you were her miracle baby? She tried about 4 times before you and imagine her surprise when she carried you to term and you were healthy. You really have her eyes, your father was my old boyfriend's golf buddy, we were like an all American sitcom. She had this long, thick jet black hair that shined and bounced around...I was always jealous of it. She was graceful and all she wanted to do was help people. Your father was determined and money hungry, they both wanted the best for you, believe me you got it. We made plans to take you and Kylah to the park after work, we never got to... She died, your father died and I thought you died as well, but here you are."

My eyes were blank, there was no surprise, hurt, shock, nothing. I couldn't even believe she would drop a bomb in me like that, had she known that I knew? I don't think she would've just said that thinking that I would act out. She talked about my mom like she was in love with her, she gazed out the window and went from being in a daze to being hurt. I couldn't control my laughter, I had to play it off like I didn't believe her.

"I don't know what you're talking about but ok whatever."

She got angry and pushed her coffee to the side.

"Listen to me, I need your help."

She leaned forward and looked me in my eyes.

"You know don't you?"

I didn't understand why one day my life was normal and the next my father wasn't my father and I wasn't myself. I leaned forward to make myself seem like I wasn't breaking.

"I don't know what you're talking about but I don't know anything, I don't know why you brought me here and I don't want to help you do anything."

I slowly guided myself back into my slouched position, continuing to look her in her eyes.

"You do, and you're hurting, and you deserve to know everything. So stop acting like you're not scared, like you don't know, and that you don't want to find out how you became Kori Tucker."

I couldn't hold it in anymore, one tear dripped down and I slapped it away. I folded my hands and said,

"What do you need me to do?"

She cracked a smile, I could tell she wanted revenge for a long time.

"Before I begin, do you have any questions?"

I thought for a moment, I could think of about 15 questions but the most important one was

"How did how did you know?"

She pulled her coffee back over infront of her and sighed.

"Well, I saw you this summer at the market, I thought my eyes were deceiving me until I saw your heart shaped birthmark on your neck. I followed you to see where you were going when I saw Martin. I knew I had to trust my gut and act fast, I unbuttoned the top button of my blouse, stood up tall and made my move. Then around the time you started school, I overheard your uncle talking about me and the relationship your mother and I had, I would've said something then but I didn't have enough evidence, and I wanted to make sure I could bury him in facts."

I guess that was a good enough answer for me, as soon as I was about to start talking Kylah text me asking me where I was.

"Kylah is texting me, should I tell her what's going on."

"No, I need her as far away from this as possible.

"We've already figured out who I was. We saw the news article, and we saw your interview with the news.

"Tell her you've made a mistake, or tell her that you changed your mind and you don't want to dig anymore. I don't want her anywhere near this, I know you may not want to lie to her but I need this one thing from you."

"If you want me to do this, I need to get back to school now, and we also need a plan to where we meet and when. I'll tell her I'm in the nurse, if we leave now I'll make it to the end of 8th period."

She agreed, payed her tab and we went on our way. During the car ride she said she needed to think of some thigs we could do to uncover the truth but I needed to continue to act normally, which I was going to do anyways. She didn't expect me to be on her side and definitely didn't expect for me to already know everything that I did. I hated knowing that I would be lying to Kylah especially after all her help, but I know it would be for the better. I hid my distance and concern and continued on. Doing this project together would kill me, and we only had two more days. A lot could happen in two days. We didn't work on it in class, we kind of just reached the surface of conversation, we had a substitute in English again and we both had study hall last period so I went to Antonio's class and she went to Chase's. It was easy acting like nothing was wrong when I was with Antonio because he always lifted my mood and he could never really tell when something was bothering me. I went straight home after school and started to think about what I was getting myself into, but I didn't care. I was ready to know the truth and take everybody down.

CHAPTER 5

I kept replaying the things Angela was saying about her and my mother's relationship. I just couldn't believe this was my life. I bust out in an uncontrollable laughter that ended in me balling my eyes out. I could feel my chest getting tight, my head was heavy and felt light headed, I fell back on my bed and struggled to keep my eyes open. I could see my younger self at the park laughing on the swing, when I looked back I saw a woman. She had long jet black hair pulled back into a pony tail. She was beautiful. She had a smile as white as the clouds, I could tell she was the sun in everybody's cloudy day. I stopped swinging and I was in her arms, I laid on her shoulders but when I looked to the side there was a man holding a camera, he disappeared behind the tree as soon as we made eye contact. I tried to yank myself out of the dream but when I opened my eyes I realized I was in another one.

The lighting in the room had a blue tint to it, there was dead silence... I could hear the cars ride by, I was laying on the bed and I couldn't move, I saw a car pull infront of the house... The stomps up the stairs got louder and louder in my ear, I tried to cover them but when I tried to move my arms I realized I was strapped to the bed. I started breathing heavily and moving rapidly trying to set myself free. When the stomping stopped the door burst open, a male figure walked slowly towards me, when I tried to speak he acted as if I wasn't there. I started screaming on the top of my lungs and the room started shaking. Before I knew it I was face to face with Antonio screaming "Baby...Baby wake up please." It took a while for my eyes to adjust, I could barely lift my head without it falling right back to the pillow. I felt like I had been drugged, I couldn't feel my body, I couldn't feel anything. When Antonio held me I felt like I was miles away.

"Baby…What were you dreaming about. You scared me half to death when the door wasn't locked and then I heard you screaming."

I looked over to notice a knife on the floor. I wanted to say something but I was lost for words. I was slightly regaining feeling in my body… Antonio kissed me over and over again, I kept moving my head every time he came close but he didn't take the hint. He just grabbed my face and forced me to look at him

"What's wrong with you?"

he said angrily, I think he was just concerned but it frightened me, he never raised his voice to me before. I just began to break down but I knew I could never tell him what was happening…

I had to think quick on my feet but my mind was still blank. I felt the dizziness kicking back in and all if a sudden I had to vomit. I had just made it to the toilet when I fell down and began to throw up. Antonio ran in behind me and held my hair. I was weak, he filled up the tub and made sure it was warm with bubbles. He brought me into my room and undressed me, I was still limp. After he put me in the tub he sat next to me and held my hand. He propped my head up with a towel so I wouldn't fall down into the tub, I still felt lightheaded and when I looked to the side I could see him going through my phone. I know he just wanted to see if I had told anyone that something was wrong but he should've been more considerate to the fact that I don't need to tell him everything. At least I thought he was looking through it until he got up and was talking to someone. I couldn't hear what he was saying, I just saw him moving around too fast and it made my head feel even worse. I got the letter "B" out before I dozed back off, I thought I was falling so I jerked back up, the water splashed everywhere. I was being lifted up before I knew it. As soon as the cooler air hit me it made my body feel so much better.

"Who were you talking to?"

I sat up in my bed and reached out my hand to grab Antonio's.

"I called your father, you're very sick, now lay back down."

My heart started racing but I couldn't show how afraid I was.

"I'm so sorry you're seeing me like this."

He just pushed my hair back and kissed my forehead. I felt no connection to him at all, it's like somebody took the form of my boyfriend… It felt like he was a stranger. I felt tears welling up in my eyes, I don't know what was happening. I heard my dad come in followed by heels hitting the porch, this is definitely not what I needed. I pretended like I drifted off to sleep in Antonio's arms before they got up to my room. I felt him slowly move from around me and began talking to my father... Martin. I tried my best to hear what they were saying but I couldn't strain my ears enough. Angela walked inside of my room and closed the door. She touched my forehead and I flinched.

"I knew you were faking."

I slapped her hand away and sat up.

"Did you drug me?"

"Forgive me but... I needed you to have another dream, I didn't expect it to take such a toll on you."

"You're sick. How did you even drug me? I didn't even drink or eat anything at the coffee shop."

My dad slowly opened the door and walked towards my bed. It was remarkable how good of an actor Angela was, it looked like true love.

"She'll be fine love." She said rubbing her hand against his cheek. You could see how much comfort he felt in her touch, he brought his hand up to hers and kissed her hand.

"Tell me if you need anything."

He said still looking deep into Angela's eyes. Before he walked out I took a glance at Martin, I felt the same empty feeling that I felt with Antonio. Like he was imposter of some sorts. I figured that it was normal considering what I just discovered but I had no idea why I felt that way towards Antonio.

When Antonio stepped back in I pretended that I still had butterflies in my stomach when I saw him, hoping they would return.

"Kylah will be here soon."

I shook my head to show him that I understood but really my mind felt like a maze with no way out of it. I tried to retrace my steps and figure out what I ate that Angela could have touched, but it literally could've been anything. Between the green apples I grab off the table every day or the lemon water I leave in the refrigerator every night so it can be ice cold in the morning. There was a weird smell to my room the other day, there were no "consume only" rules on drugging somebody right? I realized there was no point in trying to figure it out, I had more pressing matters to deal with. I was replaying my dream in my head. I figured I would be dreaming about my father soon. I started to doze off again but Antonio made sure I stayed awake long enough for me to eat whatever he was having Kylah bring me. As soon as I saw her I knew something was wrong with me. I couldn't feel anything, no happiness or relief, no connection. The same feel I had with Antonio and my father…Martin. The same emptiness that made me feel that if the room was quiet enough you would be able to hear my heart beat. The same emotionless feeling that made me rethink whether or not I had a heart. It was around 7 when everybody went their separate ways, and I was left alone. I could finally breathe. I laid in bed staring up at the ceiling, I heard my phone buzz when I turned to look I felt like I was in a maze all over again. Even my room looked unfamiliar to me. It finally hit me, all of this was never supposed to be mine. It's not mine. I don't know what it is, or who these people are.

"Who can I trust?"

I said aloud to myself. I feared looking in the mirror, I feared not being able to recognize myself. The thought of not being able understand or to feel made me so angry. I rubbed my face and began to dig my nails into my cheeks. I couldn't help it, I had an overwhelming desire to self-harm… I could feel the burning sensation, it put me at ease.

Running my fingertips against the welts that rose on my face I began to have a flash back. I remember it seemed as if time was flying and the room I was in was spinning so fast nobody in it could keep their balance. The music was growing louder in my ears and I saw men and woman in their colorful clothes, cups in hand. I shut my eyes hard and tried to remember every detail. I had a yellow teddy bear that said "Yum factory" on a button that was sewn to it… Now that I think about it I've seen the exact same teddy bear in every dream. I was a little girl again. I was crawling through the group of intoxicated grown-ups and stumbled onto the marble floor in the kitchen, it was empty until I saw a pair of brown dress shoes appear in front of me. I stumbled backwards and all sounds stopped, there was no more laughter or music that I could hear. It was unnaturally silent, like I went to an extremely high altitude and my ears started popping. I looked up but the room was still spinning, the clocks were moving faster than before and I could still see the men and woman in their colorful clothes, cups in hand. This figure hadn't budged in what could've been an hour if the clocks weren't moving so fast. I could feel myself opening my eyes until the figure kneeled down and grabbed my hand. I could feel his warmth and smell like he was standing in the room, could it have been my father? I couldn't see a face, all I had to go off of was a quick touch on my hand and a scent I couldn't out my finger on. I was trying to force myself to open my eyes but I couldn't. I could see the room slowing down along with the clocks and the men and woman didn't seem too colorful, they actually started to disappear. Next thing I knew I was in an empty space, there were no walls, floors, windows, adults with colorful clothes and drinks, even the man with the brown dress shoes disappeared. I was my current self in this

"Hello?"

I yelled out only to hear a response from my echo.

"Hello?"

I yelled louder, but this time my eyes shot open. I looked around to see what was going on but I was still alone. That didn't last for long though, a few moments later I saw my uncle…Aaron, pull into the drive way. I haven't seen him in days, I wondered what he had been doing but I forgot I didn't want to see him. I turned my light off and threw the cover over my entire body. It took him about 20 minutes to come upstairs to even check if anybody else was there.

By that time, I had to uncover my face and turn on my tv because I got hot and wasn't able to fall back to sleep. When he walked in he just stared at me. I didn't want to turn my head to look at him, since I felt disconnected with everyone else, I couldn't bring myself to look at my uncle…Aaron and notice that he seemed like an imposter as well.

"I haven't seen you in a while K crazy."

I giggled and just continued to watch commercials like they were actual shows.

"What's wrong with you?"

He said walking closer to my bed. This usually would have been the moment where I spilled the beans and told him everything, but imagine his reaction. Had I told him the truth and said

"I know my name is Cassie Powers, I know who my real parents are and I know this life wasn't supposed to be mine. I don't know why or how I came to be yours but Angela and I are plotting against the both of you."

I would just turn around and pray that he made it all make sense but I knew it wouldn't. Instead of turning that moment into a disaster I just told him I was sick. When he touched my forehead to see if I was warm I had the same feeling I did a little while ago, anger… He sat down on my bed and I could feel him staring at me. I tried my best not to look at him but I couldn't help but feel the elephant in the room trotting around like it was no tomorrow. When I finally mustered up the courage to turn my head, we made eye contact immediately.

"Your eyes are blank K..."

I could feel tears welling back up in my eyes. I felt nothing, for people that I recognize as family, friend, and lover. I didn't give much conversation to my uncle, so when he got tired of trying, I was left alone again. I sat in my room in the dark, going over everything that's happened over and over again. I tried to put my own pieces of the puzzle together, I tried answering my own questions, so I decided to go back into the room of secret photos and death certificates where this all began to make sense. I grabbed my pen with a flashlight at the end and tip toed through the dark making sure I stepped over every weak spot in our floor that made creaks. It took me almost 10 minutes to turn the handle and open the door wide enough for me to slip in without making any noise.

My uncle...Aaron never showed any violence towards me like my father did, but I would never put anything past anybody. When I finally slid my body through the slim crack in the door, I had to tack on another 10 minutes to close the door back. I clicked my flashlight and began to scan the room, I didn't know where to start, so I decided to go to the box buried in the back. My heart raced, I tried to slow down my breathing but that didn't work, I just had to try to move as swiftly as possible. I blew off the dust off the old box and started digging. I saw letters and pictures, way too many to make sense of so I decided to take the entire box. I glided across the floor like I had fairy dust sprinkled on each of my toes and snuck back to my room without so much of a hint that I had gotten up out of bed. I made up my mind to wait until Angela got here in order to go through it... This would get interesting very soon... I didn't go to school the next day because I wanted to make sure Angela and I got the privacy we needed. I knew I picked a bad day, it was Wednesday, and I knew I would have to see Kyla later today because our project was due tomorrow. I was not looking forward to it at all. I actually was a bit skeptical about continuing interactions with Angela because of the whole "drugging" thing, but I honestly had no idea how I would go about this alone. She parked around the block and ran to the door, this was the very first time I've ever seen her without heels. I expected to have a feeling of emptiness or disconnect like I had with everyone else, but she was somebody I never felt anything for in the first place.

When she walked in we didn't exchange any words. I moved slowly across the room towards the box that could potentially make our plan of destruction move forward. I began dumping everything out of the box, I could hear my heart beating with each "plop" of papers. The house was still silent, Angela made the first move to grab things off the table. As she shuffled through the items something caught my eye. A red book that was obviously old and used, strung together with brown twine. I opened it, to my surprise it was a diary. I flipped through the pages and skimmed through beautifully written cursive, until, again something caught my eye.

"Jackpot."

I said walking over to the other side of the table.

"It's a diary, it started in 1987. Written by a woman, signed by Melony Grey."

I couldn't help the overwhelming feeling I had when I heard that name.

"My mother."

I whispered. I could hear my heart beating inside of my chest and I began to sweat.

"You know your mother's name is Chasity Powers."

Angela said sternly.

"No…" I ran upstairs and shuffled through my things, Angela came in shortly after with the diary in hand.

"What are you looking for?"

She said walking closer.

"The death certificate. I know that name. This has to be the connection!"

Angela looked confused but she assisted with my search.

"Here it is."

I quickly unfolded it and scanned for the name.

"Macey Grey."

I said aloud

"Martin never told me my mother's name, he used to tell me that I shouldn't try to get close to someone I would never know. But this doesn't make sense, how did this Macey Grey character get murdered and why?"

Angela responded with a soft but scared tone,

"I have no idea, but we need to find out, and this diary is key. I want you to read through it and everything that looks important I want you to pull it out. If you can remember anything else, remember it and put these things in the best hiding place possible. Okay?"

I shook my head in agreement. I couldn't fix my lips to speak. Angela left me there to go clean up downstairs and put everything back in the box and back into the corner of the room of secrets. I paced back and forth in my room until I was tired, then sat on my bed and watched the clock. It was 1:37, school seemed like it was taking forever to let out, the longer it took for the second hand to hit the marks designated for them the more my anxiety grew. I tried to close my eyes but they snapped back open every time I did, so I just laid there. I kept staring at the jacket I wrapped up the diary in. I don't know if I was scared to read more for the simple fact that this could give me all the answers I'm looking for. In all honesty the truth is so much scarier than the lies people eat for breakfast. After a while there became an overwhelming desire to read the diary, so I finally cracked it open. I flipped through the pages before I decided to just start at the beginning. When I started I couldn't stop, I just saw words jump around the page like it was a novel coming to life. The diary began so lightly, with perfectly drawn hearts and smiley faces in the margin. I began to picture Melony as a 5'2, brown skin model type without the height aspect. I can imagine that she had a soft raspy voice that could sooth a wild herd. Her fingernails were always done and her favorite color was violet, or maybe a calm gray. She was the type to attract every kind of person and do things for herself. All of a sudden the diary turned cold. I could feel the wind brush pass my ear and goosebumps rise on my skin. It was February 28th 1989, this strong and kind woman I pictured hands quivered with every stroke of the pencil.

"Dear diary, today, Martin has become another person. He got drunk… He hit me. One time. He watched me hit the ground and stared at me with his head tilted. It seemed he viewed me as a $5,000 painting, proud of what he's just done. His eyes were hungry and I knew there was more to come. He sat down crouched down in the corner next to me and wiped the blood from my mouth. I couldn't believe it. I don't even know how to respond. Do I leave? Do I stay? Where would I go… Diary, if you have a soul please give me an answer, I pour my heart into you so you should have something for me. Xo-Melony"

CHAPTER 6

I could almost picture every detail. I bet it was raining that night. I reread the entry over and over again. I didn't stop until I got a message, it was Kylah. School was about to let out. I had to work on getting my mind right to spend this time with her. I know my dad would be home soon so I threw on my favorite black ripped jeans and a white tank top, a pair of silver earrings, my favorite necklace with a heart and simple black flats. I quickly tied my hair into a tight pony tail, grabbed my books and headed towards the library. Walking there I was pretty much in a daze. I hoped that the feelings, or lack there-of, would change now that some of the stress and confusion I felt before has lifted. Dragging my feet up the ramp to the "chill section" of the library, I caught a glimpse of a child neglecting to take candy from a stranger, it wasn't the action that caught my eye but the candy bar itself. It was a "Mr. Crisp", I couldn't help but think that this was déjà vu. I shook it off and scanned the room for Kylah, I saw her, and sitting to her left was Chase looking good as always. I waved to let them know I spotted then and jogged over to the table, as soon as I sat down Antonio came to sit right next to me.

"What is this, an intervention."

I said jokingly, but nobody laughed along.

"You haven't been in school, or returning my calls that often, you've been shutting everybody out, so they've been helping me with the finishing touches of our project."

My head snapped back in shock that this was coming from her mouth.

I couldn't be upset though, because she was right. I'd been so wrapped up in trying to put all the pieces of the puzzle together I forgot about the pieces that were already done. I inhaled deeply and said

"Well, that's good then, can I see it?"

I just decided that I would shrug it off and slowly guide things back to how they were.

"We decided to change the project all together, we don't have to discuss it, it's going to be an A."

I just shook my head because I knew Kylah was upset. I kept looking back toward the snack bar where I saw the man trying to give the girl a candy bar, but he was gone. I couldn't get it out of my head, it's like the weirdest things make a permanent indent on my brain and give me flashbacks I can't explain.

"Hey!"

I heard Antonio say in an annoyed tone.

"Yes love?"

I really need to get it together...

"Do you want to come to the party Friday night?"

I was elated that he would even invite me.

"I'm going with Chase, it'll be fun."

Kylah said, getting closer to him.

"Of course I'll go! What are we wearing?"

"Well we have to wear uniform if we're on a team so I chose to go with the basketball team." Antonio said "I want you to wear the jersey I got you."

"I'm going to wear Chase's first jersey when he joined the team freshman year, so we'll be matching. But not completely, we can't turn things into a 'who wore it best' type thing."

"I don't know.Yawl both look really good."

Chase said. I couldn't help but blush, we did have the best looking boyfriends and they obviously thought we were gorgeous.

"Don't look at my girl Chase."

Antonio said jokingly, he added

"we're going to get a limo, this is like homecoming except with all schools, where everybody who's anybody will be there."

I got nervous because I knew I would be representing Antonio, everybody knew him, he was one of the most popular boys everywhere.

"Don't worry about paying for anything, Antonio and I got it."

Chase said.

"Just focus on looking good and make sure yawl parents say it's ok, the party goes all night."

We shook our heads knowing they wouldn't say no.

"You two drink right?" he added.

Kylah and I both looked at each other and said

"We can that night."

Chase began to say

"But isn't Ha-..." until Antonio shook his head a few times and told him to cut it.

"Isn't what?"

I tried to think about what he could've been saying, but Kylah said it for me.

"Haley. Haley Price is going to be there."

Antonio threw his hands up in the air and smacked his teeth.

"I knew that already, so what?"

Antonio grabbed my face to focus on him.

"Baby please, don't fight, argue or pay any attention to her. Please I'm begging you."

I rolled my eyes.

"Why are you so protective of somebody you're not with anymore. Plus, you should be telling *her* not to mess with *me*."

"She's right bro." Chase said shrugging his shoulders.

"Okay Kori, I'll tell her. I just really don't want you to beat her up. She won't stop coming after you." I let out a sigh and changed the subject all together, "I'm about to go order some food, can you give me money?"

"I'll go with you."

Kylah said with her hand out towards Chase. Both Chase and Antonio pulled a wad of cash out of their pockets. Antonio handed me 100 dollars in 20's and Chase gave Kylah a 50.

"What do you think I'm about to order?"

I always knew he had money but I didn't know it was like that, I definitely didn't know Chase had loaf either.

"I gave it to you so you wouldn't be mad at me. Get me some boneless wings."

He said pulling out my chair. Kylah walked around the table and we walked over to the café. We had simple conversation and went back over to the table with food for everyone. Chase and Antonio had to go run a few errands for the party so Antonio dropped Kylah and I off at the nail salon, we both got another 50.

CHAPTER 7

After getting a manicure and pedicure we headed back to my place, which I'm glad was not far from there. When we walked in both my dad...Martin and Angela was there, so we killed two birds with one stone. Of course they said we can go so we ran upstairs to plan our outfits.

"So what are you going to do if Haley actually does say something to you."

I shrugged my shoulders.

"I'm going to be too worried about Antonio, I'll leave her alone like he told me to."

We just left the conversation there. I went downstairs to get some snacks while we watched a movie, when I came back, she was reading the diary.

"What are you doing?"

I said trying to snatch it from her.

"Who is this?"

she said running to the other side of the room. I dropped the snacks and ran over to her.

"Stop, just drop it ok?"

She threw the book across the room and pushed me.

"Are you serious! You haven't let me in on anything! I dealt with you while you cried, I helped you put two and two together. Who is this! Why are you shutting me out now?"

I could feel tears welling up in my eyes, I wanted nothing more than for her to be up to speed, but Angela said no.

"I don't know whose diary that is Kylah."

She grabbed her things and ran out the door. A few minutes later Angela came into my room.

"What did you do?"

"Nothing, she found the diary and she's mad I didn't tell her what was going on. She was the one that helped me find out who I *actually* am."

"And who are you? Kori?" my father...Martin said slowly walking into the room."

"Nobody baby, it's a girl thing, trying to figure out who she is as a teenager, you know how it is."

Angela replied quickly. As I watched him as he continued walking. I can see how concentrated he was, trying not to stumble.

"You've been drinking?"

I said taking a few steps back. He started to laugh and then his face got serious. He stumbled up to me and leaned on my bed and grabbed my hair with his other hand.

"What are you doing!"

Angela said as she rushed over to my side. The hand he was using for support swung back and hit Angela in the face. He lost his balance and I fell down with him. I began kicking and screaming and trying to release myself from his grip.

"Angela!"

I said reaching towards her hand. I could tell she was in shock. This was it, she finally saw what I witnessed my entire life. He started laughing again,

"You look just like your mother..."

His head snapped back to see Angela standing, wiping blood from her lip. He let go of my hair and got onto his knees.

"I am so sorry... I'm so sorry..."

He said it over and over again until Angela joined him on his knees and began to rock him.

"It's ok, you didn't mean it."

I couldn't help but show the disgust on my face, I rubbed my head and hoped a chunk of hair didn't fall on the ground next to me. I listened to him sob and mouthed the words *you ok?* to Angela. She shook her head and began to rise slowly, for a second time. My father...Martin following shortly after. I wondered what was going through Angela's head now, was she still willing to help me, or was she going to call a quits? I realize now that I can't afford to lose Kylah as a friend over this. I don't even know why I thought I could keep this integral part of my life secret from her. Especially now that she made a good point by saying she's the one that brought me to this realization. All of a sudden I got a text from Antonio saying his parents were gone for the night and asked me if I wanted to sleep over, I jumped at the chance to get out of this house. I tried to call Kylah about three times before I gave up, so after I got my things together for the night and school tomorrow. I asked Antonio to take me over to her house before we headed to his. I left the house quietly, I was surprised at the chilly weather, I guess it fit the mood perfectly. When I got in the car Antonio looked good as always.

"I have a surprise for you."

He said excitedly.

"What is it?"

I saw him fidgeting with something behind his neck, I wasn't even thinking that he would be grabbing one of his gold chains that he never took off.

"I've been thinking about this for a while…"

he said as he put the chain with the #3 that twirled inside a basketball around my neck, "but I have 3 chains and it's only right that I give my number one girl, my #3." I laughed at his cheesiness but I was so excited.

"You always talk about how much these mean to you, are you sure you want to give this to me?"

He smiled, leaned over and kissed me slowly

"you mean a lot to me, you deserve it. Now, what happened with you and Kylah?"

It was so much of a relief that Antonio had nothing to do with any of the craziness, I loved that our relationship could be simple.

"It's just a little fight, can you take me to her house really quick? I need to patch things up with her."

When I turned to put my seatbelt on my face started to sting, when I hit the ground my face must have scraped the carpet. I knew once Antonio saw it he would ask what happened, I wonder how he would react if I began to tell him all the years of abuse I actually dealt with.I'd rather just keep it to myself. I dreaded having to tell Kylah that I've been sneaking around with Angela and I dreaded even more having to tell her the events that happened shortly after she left, but I felt like this was the only way to save our relationship.

"While you're at Kylah's I'm going to pick up James and Chris alright?" Antonio said pulling up to the house.

"Ok, wait until I'm inside to pull off."

I ran over and knocked on the door a few times and waited a couple seconds, I went to knock again when Chase opened the door with no shirt on. My eyes shot open when I saw Kylah walk up to the door without hers on either.

"What do you want."

"We need to talk, can I come in?"

"No. You have one minute." She said, grabbing her robe off the chair.

"Kylah, you know we have more issues than to be discussed in one minute."

"What's going on between you two?" Chase said putting a t-shirt and then a hoodie on after.

"Why don't you go with Antonio to pick up James and Chris?"

Chase shrugged his shoulders and ran over to join him in the car, I waved to Antonio to give him the ok to leave and I pushed passed Kylah to get into the door.

"You want to be mad? Ok fine, but your mom has known this entire time, the only reason she's with my dad is to get close to me. She told me not to involve you because she didn't want you to get hurt...The diary that you were reading belongs to Macey Grey, the woman I thought was my mother when I found her death certificate. It's not, all I know is she dated my father and wrote about a lot of things that happened with them. Your mom and I have been planning to meet up more often to try to put pieces together by finding things in our extra room that will bring us any closer to finding out the truth..."

Kylah began to say something when I cut her off,

"There's something else... After you left, Angela came to my room to ask me what happened, my dad was drunk and had one of his episodes. He hit Angela and dragged me to the floor."

Kylah just stood there in shock. I walked over to her slowly and hugged her. I could tell how hurt and tense she was, she didn't say anything, just hugged me back. When she looked at my face she lightly touched the brush burn,

"You're bleeding."

"I'll be fine, Angela is fine too, maybe shaken up a bit but she's ok... Are we ok?"

I looked deep into hereyes, they were empty, just like mine...I feared this would happen, I just hope the light can be brought back into her.

"We're ok."

Kylah's voice cracked, she cleared her throat quickly and stood up straight. I heard a honk outside and saw Chase jog up to the door.

"Carry on." I said rubbing my hand against her face and heading to the door.

"Bye Chase!"

I said as I shook myself out of my funk and ran to the car, I was so glad Antonio told James and Chris to sit in the back. "What's up boys." I said looking back and waving.

"Damn. What you do to her Ant?" Chris said. The lights began to dim.

"Nothing! Shut up."

"What do you mean?" Antonio said flipping the light back on. "Baby what happened to your face!"

"Don't make a scene."

"Yo, are you serious? It looks like somebody slid your face down a wall! I know damn well it wasn't Kylah!"

I quickly turned the music up. "You need to drive, now."

"We're not done talking about this."

Antonio sped off quickly and dropped off the boys at their houses and drove to his. It was just now hitting 9:30 but I was exhausted. I could tell Antonio was mad and was not going to let this go. We walked in the house and despite his anger he still took off my shoes and coat and proceeded to carry me up the stairs without a word.

"So what happened to your face Kori?"

Antonio said walking into his room.

"My dad hit me Antonio. He was drunk and he hit me."

I saw the shock and disappointment in his face.

"Please do not pity me, I don't want to talk about it, ok? I've been dealing with this all my life and I would really appreciate it if we can keep it out of conversation. I'm really tired anyways, just lay with me?"

He took off everything but his shorts and helped me change into my pajamas.

"We're going to go get breakfast in the morning so we'll be late to school. Are you hungry now?"

he said pushing my hair to the back. I shook my head no, a few moments later Antonio said "I am." With a mischievous smile. He kissed me softly then began to slide down under the covers and take care of me. The next thing I remember is rolling over and realizing I fell asleep. Before I opened my eyes I heard Antonio whispering but had an angry tone. I kept my eyes closed and moved closer to the right side of the bed to hear better. I barely heard the other side of the conversation so I had to fill in the blanks for the most part.

"I can't believe you would try to flip this on me!"

Antonio got quiet for a while, I assumed the female voice I heard was Haley. She raised her voice every few words and then goes back down. The next thing that came out Antonio's mouth surprised me the most and made me sure of who was on the other end. He said,

"I didn't shove the multiple shots down your throat! I get that your parents were splitting up and your mom was running away with another man, you felt like she wasn't the mother you grew up with, so you took it upon yourself to get rid of being a mother. When you made that choice alone, you made a choice for me to no longer be a father."

He raised his voice and got up from the bed.

"You were three months! Did you not think that regularly drinking wouldn't cause a miscarriage? Don't even answer that because I bet you did it on purpose!"

I felt sick, I couldn't believe what I was hearing. They had a baby. All this time Kylah and I thought they broke up because she tried to hook up with Chase. I kept my eyes closed and made sure I could hear as much as possible.

"It doesn't matter, I told you I would stay and help you."

Antonio began to sniffle and I can tell that he was crying, he threw himself on the chest in front of his bed.

"I tried to love you... I-I would've loved you..."

His voice began to crack. I could feel my heart dropping into my stomach and my eyes began to burn.

"Listen to me, I forgave you a long time ago, I just don't want anything to do with you. I love Kori, you hear that? *Love*, and you will never mess that up. I'm bringing her to this party and swear to God if you mess with her I'm going to tell everyone why you really went to that mental hospital."

He quickly hung up the phone a threw it against the wall. When it made the loud thud it gave me an excuse to pretend like I was finally waking up. I tossed and turned a few times before I said anything, by that time Antonio was already crawling up next to me and kissing me all over my face.

"Baby what time is it?"

"It's 12:41."

"Who were you on the phone with baby?"

I said sitting up and stretching. I didn't even know if I wanted to hear him admit it I just wanted to see if he would, I'm definitely afraid to push it though.

"You do know I love you right?"

Antonio grabbed me and pulled me on top of him. I couldn't help but smile and push what I just heard in the back of my head.

"I love you more baby." I said "Who were you talking to? Or was I dreaming?"

"You must've been dreaming. I've just been sitting here."

I thought a bit more, I didn't know whether or not it was my business. At least I know he hasn't been with her and that he actually did love me. At that moment I convinced myself that I didn't care if he told me or not. We just laid together and talked about the future and some of the past. Of course I had a habit of dodging questions that had anything to do with my father...Martin, I couldn't even shake the need to do it or to have an honest and open relationship with Antonio....

CHAPTER 8

I did learn, however that his mother miscarried a few times before April was born. A healthy baby at that. I guess I could understand why his anger is so deep for Haley after she brought the loss onto herself purposely. He's always been popular in school and he never thought of doing anything other than going into a professional sport because that's what everyone expected him to do. He said that the more he thought about it, the more he realized he would want to be a grief counselor, or one of the people who deliver babies.

This was the first time Antonio ever opened up about something he thought that was below the surface, the kind of thinking that consumes a mind or has a person dreaming about it. I didn't mean to but I couldn't hold it anymore.

"I heard you talking on the phone Antonio. I know what happened between you and Haley."

I continued to lay on his chest without moving, Antonio didn't budge and he didn't get tense, he was surprisingly calm.

"You want to know what used to keep me up at night K?"

He said continuing the long solid stroke up and down my back.

"It was rain. That might sound stupid but, it was raining the day I walked into the kitchen and sat down at the breakfast table right before I saw blood dripping down from my mother's leg. It's the rain drops sliding down the window in the hospital room when my mom lost the baby for the third time. It seemed like with every drop of rain another tear dropped from my father's eyes... you know he taught me never to cry? When Haley wasn't returning my phone calls I thought she was just mad at me, but when I started asking around they said they heard a nasty split up between her mom and dad was happening and I was shocked that I was hearing it via locker room talk..."

He sighed and smacked a tear from his face.

"I didn't know she was pregnant you know... All I got was a drunken call telling me that it worked, that he or she, as she put it, was gone. Concerned I rushed over there to see vodka bottles and old shot glasses scattered around her room. She made it to sleep quickly, when I walked over to the bed I knew something was wrong, other than the obvious. I threw back the covers to get in bed with her when I saw blood on the sheets."

I sighed and reached for his hand, he snatched it away.

"Tell me about your father."

I was thinking about being hesitant or ignoring the question, instead of just coming out like a rehearsed line I thought about what I was saying. I was really just trying to figure out how far I actually wanted to go with this conversation.

"He gets drunk, he hits me. That's all there is to it."

"How long?" Antonio replied quickly.

"Around 3 or 4 years now, he's not always bad, but he flares up months at a time."

"You ever thought about running away?"

I took a pause... If I did run away, that would pretty much move things along, maybe not in the direction I need it to but then again it could work out perfectly. I don't even know what the "right or wrong" way was.

"Do you?"

I glanced over at the clock and noticed it was still only pushing 1:30. I noticed Antonio falling asleep but I couldn't help but ask

"Why didn't you love her?"

I looked up at him but he continued to stare deep into the ceiling.

"I don't know." Antonio said rolling over. "I really don't..."

I just left it there and let myself drift to sleep with him... I had another dream about my childhood, my mind went right back to the man trying to give the little girl a Mr. Crisp bar. In my dream I was around 4 or maybe I just turned 5. I was running through an aisle trying to find my mother, I assume, when I bumped into a man. When I looked up to see who it was, it was Martin, with a huge smile on his face, he kneeled down next to me and grabbed my hand.

"Do you want a candy bar Cassie?"

He said holding out the Mr. Crisp bar. I shook my head no and ran away. I couldn't make out my parents' face, and that was killing me. During the ride home inside of the dream, I looked out the window to see Martin again, in the car next to me, he looked over, smiled and waved. A few moments later he reached out his arms and grabbed me out of the car, I jerked myself awake and immediately got out of the bed. Surprisingly Antonio didn't get up, it was 5:00am.I had an hour and a half before his alarm went off so I decided to shower.I knew Antonio wanted to go out for breakfast but I decided to cook for him instead. After my shower I slipped on one of Antonio's shirts and started cooking. I made blueberry waffles, Antonio's favorite, sausage links, a few spicy steak omelets and a large glass of orange juice. I made him a beautiful plate and laid it on a tray and took it up to him. It was only 6:15 now. I was glad he was still asleep, I kissed him lightly and watched him open his eyes slowly.

"Surprise baby."

I said laying the food and juice down on the dresser next to his bed.

"What is all this for?"

"To show my love and dedication to you."

"I see you made yourself comfortable, you look better in my shirts than I do. You should wear that to school."

Antonio said laughing and rubbing his face.

"You know I would rather you take this off."

I said in a sexy tone.

"That's all you want me for isn't it? Let me eat my food geez."

I rolled my eyes and gave him the plate, he ate the whole thing in less than 10 minutes.

"How did you just eat that so fast? You're a bottomless pit."

He tossed the plate to the side and chugged the orange juice down. He leaned over to kiss me but I pushed him away.

"Bye, go shower."

"Why, you don't like my morning nastiness?"

He pulled me closer and kissed me all over my face

"Come on, let's just skip school baby."

"I can't, Kylah and I have our presentation today. Now get up, shower and get dressed."

"Mm, I like it when you get all commando on me. Okay, I'll go. Pick out my outfit, make me look good."

As soon as the bathroom door closed the alarm sounded, I turned it off and put my hair into a bun. Antonio had a walk in closet, inside were built in shelves with a long line of his watches, chains, earrings and pinky rings. I looked around and picked out a simple black shirt, his dark designer jeans with a gold trim, both his chains, his gold watch with a black face and his gold pinky ring with the matching earring. I walked over to the back of the closet to pick out his shoes, since I was wearing my timberlands I figured he should wear his too. After I laid everything out on the bed I heard the shower turn off and Antonio came out of the fog.

"Put a towel on."

I couldn't keep my eyes off of him or my mind out of the gutter.

"I see you didn't get dressed. Come here."

I walked over to him slowly, trying to stop myself from blushing too hard. He picked me up effortlessly and pinned me to the wall.

"This is all you want me for?"

He said with a smile. I looked down and watched him bring me closer to him, anticipating a kiss I closed my eyes, only for them to shoot back open when I felt him push inside. He watched me react, his eyes locked to mine. My body pressed against his and my nails dug into his back. I felt the steam continue to poor out of the bathroom, it seemed like it stuck to our skin. He snatched me from the wall and continued to pull me up and down all the way to the bed. He laid me down and completely changed his pace. It turned slow, and passionate. He grabbed my hands and held them above my head, he kissed me as we finished together.

"Yeah, that's what I love you for."

I said wiping myself down, watching Antonio do the same. He chuckled.

"Yeah, I know, get dressed so we can go now. I like the outfit you picked out for me too."

I put on my clothes, Antonio's chain, hoop earrings and a watch.

"I don't know how many times I'm going to tell you to stop wearing leggings and half shirts, especially together."

"Does it matter?"

"Yes it matt-... Never mind, it doesn't, everybody knows you're my girl anyways. I see you don't have any rings. That has to change."

"Is this your way of saying you're about to put a ring on it?"

I said grabbing his light blue button up shirt I had on before and put it back on.

"Yes, I am. That looks so much better by the way." He said putting two stacks of money in a clip. "Hand me my keys and let's go."

I grabbed they keys off the dresser and followed him out the door. It was 8:00 now, 15 minutes until school opened.

"I have to make a stop first alright?"

I shrugged my shoulders and turned up the radio. After a while we pulled up to a house deep in the hood. I was caught off guard and confused.

"Come on." Antonio said opening my door. "It'll just take a second."

I stepped out the car and quickly buttoned up the shirt.

"Where are we?"

Antonio knocked three times before somebody cracked the door open. "Who is it?"

"Man watch out Kells, it's Skinner."

"Who you with?"

Antonio grabbed my hand and pushed through the door,

"Man watch out. You're acting like you Monsters' security detail."

He moved through to the back of the house. There were men everywhere, smoking, drinking, playing dice. I was shocked, I had no idea Antonio had this side to him, and who the hell was Skinner? I thought to myself.

"You alright baby?" Antonio said letting go of my hand.

"Yeah I'm cool."

I tried to be as calm as possible but I was freaking out in my head. Antonio started walking and I grabbed on to the back of his shirt. He turned around quickly and moved my hand. That's when I saw an outline of a gun.

"Antonio?"

I said with a shaky voice. He ignored me, we finally got to whatever room we were on our way to and Antonio knocked on the door again.

"Curry, it's Skinner. Open up."

The door opened quickly and we walked in. It was exactly how I imagined, a fat guy with 5 or 6 chains sitting at a big desk with money all around, drugs and guys with bulges in their pants that I doubt were coming from excitement. A tall and skinny boy with dreads came from the corner of the room and stood behind me. He put his lips to my ear and my body froze.

"I like short girls."

He said pressing against me. I squeezed Antonio's hand and he turned around to say something when he saw him. He pulled the gun from his pants and pointed it at him. He walked closer and pressed it to his head.

"What's up with you slim? You see she with me right?"

I could see the sweat rising on his skin.

"No problem skinner, my bad I didn't know it was like that."

"Pop." Antonio said as he shifted the gun to his chest. "Pop. Pop."

He backed "slim" or whoever he was into a wall.

"Understood?" Antonio said putting the gun back into his pants.

He just shook his head and put his hands up. The man sitting at the desk started to laugh hysterically.

"Come here girl."

He said waving his hand at me. I looked back at Antonio and he nodded, giving me the ok to go.

"I'm guessing you never saw this side of him huh?"

I shook my head no and fought back a tear.

Antonio walked up to us. "I'm sorry, but this is me, a part of me anyways. This is not gone change us."

My mind was running a mile a minute, I didn't know if it changed the way I viewed him or not. I don't know if liked it, I just knew I didn't want to lose him. Did I really care what he did during his free time?

"I knew the money wasn't coming from trees, I just didn't know you were pull out a gun type."

The big man laughed.

"Oh yeah, she's a keeper." I smiled and he slapped me up, I felt in, I felt accepted. It was somewhat of a good feeling.

"So what you got for me?"

Antonio said pulling me back over to his side.

"You did really good these few weeks Skinner. So check this out, I'm about to have a grand dropped off to you, and I'm about to give shorty a band. You want that?"

I was shocked.

"Me?"

The big man laughed again and opened the drawer next to him. There was nothing but hundred dollar bills getting thrown on the desk. He started counting it and put it in a rubber band. He reached across and held it in front of me.

"Yeah, you."

I took it out his hand and he nodded at Antonio.

"It'll be dropped off to you."

We both said bye and walked out, on our way through the house Chase called out to him.

"Yo, let me come with yawl!"

He said jogging over to us.

"You too? I was just completely in the dark. I take it Kylah is too?"

Chase shrugged his shoulders.

"Yo call Kylah tell her we about to pick her up." Antonio said pulling off.

Chase called her and we all went to school, we only missed first period so that was good.We walked in and went our separate ways. I couldn't stop thinking about the events from this morning, all the way back to the dream I had. I threw myself into my school work to try to keep my mind off of it. While I was in class I dropped my pen and I rolled up to the front of the room, when I leaned over to get to get it, the stack of money fell out my bra. Of course everybody made a scene so by lunch everybody was talking about it. It's not fun hearing whispers in the hall knowing they're about you.

"What's up Kori, I mean the female plug."

Kylah joked as we met up at the door of our English class.

"Shut up." I said rolling my eyes and walking to my seat.

"I just want to get this class over with, this day really."

We took our seats and waited to be called up for our presentation but it never came, we all just had to hand the project in because we had to take a surprise state pre-test which was good for me because I was not in the mood. The day finished fairly quickly and I just couldn't wait to get home.

CHAPTER 9

Antonio met me at my last class so we could walk out of school together, I couldn't keep my eyes off of him. This athletic, tall, muscular, funny, smart and charming guy... Is hood, and not just any hood, he is the thing that goes bump in the night, to me, anyways.

"I heard about that little incident in your class room."

"Yeah." I said pushing a few strands of stray hair back into my bun. "It was embarrassing."

"How? This literally bumps you up to one of the most popular girls in school."

"I thought I already was."

I said with a chuckle. I saw Antonio a few different sides of Antonio today. I kept replaying the cute and corny boyfriend, to the erotic side all the way to the thug side.

"So, do you always have that gun around? Why did it take you this long to show me that side of you? What do you do? Sell drugs? Does this mean I'm completely in? What do I have to do for this money? Wait... What does Chase do?"

I badgered him with questions so quick he struggled to answer them all.

"Yes, I wanted you to like the nice side of me first. I am the hit man, no, yes, and nothing I did it for you. I can take you shopping before the party if you want, with my money though I want you to keep that. Chase is a drug dealer for Curry. He's supply, I'm demand"

"A hit man? Antonio, you've killed people?"

My nails stabbed the inside of my palm, I could feel my heart beat.

"Baby. Don't ask me questions you don't want the answer to."

"I do want the answer. I want to know."

"Raegan Walter. Bryan Chandler. Mia Taylor. Darion Smith. Alex Lincoln. Carlton Valdez. Cameron Holtz. Their blood is on my hands."

I was shocked, I was expecting a number, not a personalized list.

"So, when he said you did good last week?"

"I didn't kill anybody, but I beat up a few guys and got his money from them. That's it. It's been two months since..."

"But-." I began.

"Make this your last question Kori."

Antonio said sternly. I thought long and hard before I opened my mouth again.

"Do you, um. Do you enjoy it?"

He shrugged his shoulders, but I saw a smirk come across his face.

"It's alright."

"Antonio, look at your face! You have smirk planted there like you're reliving a childhood memory!"

He shook his head and pulled over. I pushed him,

"A smirk Antonio!" I said pushing him again. I looked at him with lost eyes, tears came flowing down like a stream. Antonio couldn't even look at me.

"Baby I- I can't-."

Antonio started throwing punches at the wheel.

"WHY DID YOU ASK ME KORI? WHY!"

I was so afraid. I don't know if he was angry or hurt. Angry because I asked, or hurt because he was monster. *He is a monster.* I snapped myself out of the thought quickly.

He reached his arm over to touch me and I flinched. He punched the wheel 3 more times in a row, when his hand started to bleed he got out the car and slammed the door so hard I thought the window cracked. I took out the keys and anticipated getting out of the car for a moment. I told myself over and over that he was still the person that I love, until I made myself believe it was true.

"I'm so sorry. This is all just a huge shock, and when it didn't seem to bother you I just I-I don't know."

I grabbed his hand and led him back into the car.

"You can't leave me, you can't."

Antonio said, holding my hand tighter and kissing it repeatedly. "Come on, let's go."

He lagged behind me and pulled off without another word. The entire ride home I sunk deeper in my seat, every time I would look over another tear drop from Antonio's face. Blood continued to flow from the cuts on his hands and his shoulders were drooping. Where I once saw this strong, able bodied man, I now saw a weakness. *Me.* I thought to myself. How could I break down this unremorseful killer? This person that was once a player? I pushed the thoughts out of my head as I walked into the house after kissing Antonio good bye.

As soon as I walked in I could tell the vibe was different. I pushed the feeling to the back of my head and walked up stairs to my room. I threw my things down, and laid on my bed. I got a few moments of peace before I shot back up.

"Wait."

I said standing up. I walked out into the hallway. *What is it?* I couldn't shake the feeling. I turned back around and studied my room, everything seemed to be in-tact. I ran over to my dresser and reached my hand under it to make sure the diary was still there, it was. I got back up and rubbed my face.

"What is it brain!"

I yelled to myself, getting aggravated. I walked back out of my room and walked slowly through the hall way. I walked passed the extra room, to the stairs, peeked in my fathers' room then turned around to head back. Taking another glance at the extra room, I saw it. My heart was beating out of my chest and I ran to my room to call Angela.

"Hello?" She says nonchalantly, like her voice usually is.

"He knows."

"He knows what? How do you know?" There was nothing but panic in her voice.

"I don't know what he knows, or thinks he knows, but there's a padlock on the extra rooms' door Angela."

The other side of the phone went silent. I just hoped she was still breathing over there.

"Hello?" I said nervously. "Are you there?"

I dropped the phone when I saw a figure appear in the door. My head snapped to the side and my heart fell.

"Oh, hi uncle Sandy."

"Where's Martin?"

He said sternly, I felt as if this was a business meeting, there was no love coming from him like it usually is. I shrugged my shoulders.

"Who were you talking to?"

"Kylah, my friend, our phones must have disconnected or something."

I fought with myself in my head to whether or not I should ask about the lock on the door. I decided against it because then I would have to explain my sudden interest of what's inside. All of a sudden my body felt heavy. I felt a sharp pain in my head that made me fall onto my bed.

"What's wrong?"

Uncle Sandy said rushing to my side. Even though he was concerned, the transaction was still cold.

"Nothing, leave me, it's just a migraine." I said pushing him away. "Shut my door too."

I got up and closed my curtains so minimum light would shine through. I took off my clothes, put on my robe and climbed into bed. As soon as I got comfortable enough to close my eyes Kylah called. I let it go to voice mail. A few moments later I got a text from her saying that she was coming over right after school to get ready for the party tomorrow. I didn't respond. I closed my eyes tightly in hopes that would make me go to sleep faster, but all it did was make images of Antonio holding a gun to someone's head appear. If that wasn't enough, my mind didn't spare me the grim details of him actually pulling the trigger. I couldn't tell whether or not I was dreaming, day dreaming or just having very vivid thoughts. I no longer could open my eyes, and I felt glued to the bed. My mind surpassed all of the things that would usually make a person panic and I began to let my thoughts loose.

How long had he been killing? Does Kylah know Chase is a drug dealer? Why did Haley kill the baby? Why is there a padlock on the door? Who put it there? What am I going to do with this money? Can I really get over what I know about Antonio? What is this party going to be like? What do my dreams mean?

It seemed almost as if this was my body's way of saying I was going through too much…putting myself through too much. My mind must have been shut down for a while because I slowly began to feel myself slip into a dream.

I was riding with Antonio after he left basketball practice.

"Babe, we should go out to eat after your shower, I know you worked hard at practice so you deserve dinner."

Antonio grabbed my hand.

"Sounds like a plan, but we're going back to my house for desert."

I started to blush, I couldn't hide how much I liked that idea. Suddenly I felt glass cut into my body and I watched it fly everywhere. The car began to serve and spin wildly.

"Antonio!"

I screamed frantically as the car smashed into a telephone pole. Everything went black for a moment and when I woke I was in a horrible amount of pain. My right arm felt like it had been shredded into a thousand pieces. I looked over to the drivers' side but I didn't see Antonio.

"Where is he?"

I lifted my head and looked through the passenger's rear view mirror to see Antonio smashing a man's head into the concrete.

"Stop! Please! I won't speed again! I-I learned my lesson." He screamed "I'll give you anything you want."

He sounded so frantic that it sent chills down my spine.

"Antonio sto-..."

My voice was drowned out by a gun shot. The man laid there gripping his bleeding shoulder.

"You almost killed me and my girlfriend!"

I watched Antonio stand over him.

"Please, let me live!"

Antonio didn't listen, he aimed the gun at his chest. 'pop, pop' the gun shots filled the air. He aimed the gun again, this time at his head. 'Pop' the final shot left him lifeless. I wanted to scream, but when I saw the smirk on Antonio's face I stopped. He really was a monster. Antonio walked back over to the car and gently pulled me out. I finally spoke, disregarding the pain I was in.

"Why would you kill him? Why! It was an accident. You know he didn't mean it!"

Tears rolled down my face, with every tear my face stung. Antonio seemed to be taken back by my anger. Another smirk was planted across his face.

"I'm a monster, remember?"

The world crashed down around me as I heard those words. I quickly pushed myself out of his arms and I fell back onto the concrete. I began to crawl away, expecting Antonio to follow me, I looked back only to see him continuing to stand there. I saw the ambulance coming around the corner, I looked back to call for Antonio when I saw him holding the gun to his head.

"Sorry Kori."

Antonio said right before he pulled the trigger. That gunshot was the loudest. I felt my heart drop, next thing I knew I was passed out again.

CHAPTER 10

I woke up on the floor of my room with a migraine. The nightmare felt so real, I didn't know what to think of it.

"I'm a monster, *remember?*"

The words that poured out of Antonio's mouth echoed in the back of my head. Suddenly my phone began to vibrate under my thigh, I grabbed it quickly and saw that it was Antonio, I let it go to voicemail. I wasn't mad at him, but after the events of the day I needed time to breath. I tossed my phone on the bed and stood up slowly. I caught a glimpse of my face in the mirror, it was stained with tears and my cheeks were puffy. *Antonio is the person I fell in love with.* I thought to myself, I couldn't believe I had that horrible dream about him. I slid back into my bed slowly, I was still in pain from the dream. It was only 9:30 so I laid motionless for a half an hour, when I started to drift back to sleep I sat up and decided to call Antonio. I'm going to try to avoid having another nightmare. His phone went straight to voicemail, after I hung up I just let my phone drop,

"My boyfriend is someone that enjoys killing."

I whispered to myself. I tried to understand it, but saying it out loud only made my reality come to life. I think it was his smirk, how could he smile... My thoughts were cut short when Kylah called, I picked up on the first ring.

"Hey, sorry I didn't respond I went to sleep as soon as I got home."

"Don't worry about it, anyways, you excited for the party?"

"Yeah I am." I said, remembering Haley was going to be there, and what I found out about her. "I just don't want to upset Antonio because of Haley."

"Girl, if she pops off I'll do something so Antonio can't be mad at you."

"You won't have to Ms. Tough Guy."

I said sarcastically. I heard Chases' voice in the background.

"What are yawl doing with each other so late?"

Kylah laughed.

"Bye Kori."

She hung up, I felt alone again. I tried Antonio again, it went to voice mail again. I got up and walked around the house, nobody was home. I have no idea where my father…Martin has been. I shrugged it off and ran back to my room to read more of the diary. I flipped through pages when something caught my eye.

"Ever since I lost the baby, Martin has been so distant. He won't touch me, won't look at me and he definitely won't stop drinking. I thought that we would be closer after our baby girl died, but he's fascinated with other people's children now. He's been spending more time with Aaron, I don't know why. I pray that the Martin I fell in love with will come back to me. I'll be back tomorrow diary. Xoxo Macey."

"So much for that." I said aloud. "Martin isn't capable of love."

I thought about what she said though.

"he's fascinated with other people's children now." Could that have been a stressor for him. Is that how he found me? Was Martin stalking me? I felt like I was reaching, trying too hard to put two and two together, but it made perfect sense. Was my uncle…Aaron helping? I continued to flip through the diary when a photo slipped out and fell onto the bed. The back read, *"The Power family, 1992."* I flipped it over, it was my mom and dad…It was me in the photo. Tears wouldn't stop running down my face. My mother was beautiful, my father was strong and handsome, I looked so happy. I wiped my tears from my face and searched for the page the photo fell from. I flipped through pages, Macey whined about how fat she'd gotten, how long it took at the grocery store, it didn't even seem like the same person was writing.

"Something must've happened."

I said aloud, still flipping through the pages. I heard patter on the window, I threw back my curtains and looked outside.

"It's the rain."

I thought about Antonio, then my thoughts shifted over to myself. I remember the article saying that a slippery road caused the accident that supposedly killed me and my family. It only took a few moments for the light rain to turn to pouring rain. I called Antonio again. This time he picked up.

"Hello?"

"Did you see it?"

I said with a shaky voice. I heard him sigh.

"Yeah, I'm looking at it now."

"Can I see you?"

There was a long pause.

"I don't really think you want to do that, I just- I just um… I did that-."

I cut him off, I pretended he was going to say something non malicious, like I just baked a cake or I just blew bubbles with my little sister April.

"Please, I don't want to hear it. You don't have to tell me, just come get me."

I said it with conviction, like I really didn't care. I did.

"I'll be there in about an hour. Bye for now."

I hung up, still staring outside watching the rain fall. I brushed off all my emotions and thoughts and started getting ready. I got three texts back to back. Two were from Kylah saying

"That moment when Chase has to leave." A few seconds later she said "I'm so bored now."

I wondered where he went so quickly. I also got a text from Antonio saying

"I'm going to pick you up right now, we have to go see Curry though."

I rolled my eyes, and replied to Kylah first.

"Where did he have to go in such a rush?"

As I waited for a reply Antonio texted me again saying he was outside. I grabbed a hoodie and walked out the door and got into the car.

"What's up baby."

"Hey."

I said putting on my seatbelt. I tried not to look at him for a second, but he grabbed my face and made me.

"Are we good?"

"Depends, did you completely wash the blood off your hands?"

"There was no blood, I snappedJohn's neck. Now are you done being petty?"

I was shocked, but I guess it was time for me to stop acting surprised.

Antonio isn't hiding himself from me anymore, I just have to accept that. I rolled my eyes.

"Whatever."

I said as Antonio pulled off. The drive was silent. I didn't even turn on the radio. We pulled up to Curry's house and Antonio leaned over to grab his gun out of the glove compartment. He only took the one out of the four that was inside.

"Can I have one?"

Antonio looked at me like he was confused or didn't understand what I was saying.

"Um, for what?"

"I don't know." I said grabbing the gun with the silencer attached to it. "Bonnie and Clyde?"

Antonio smacked his teeth.

"Man, put that gun down and get out the car. You aren't a shooter, you're a rider."

I laughed, I couldn't believe this was normal conversation. Walking up to the house Kylah responded to me.

"He had to go to his grandmother's house, she needed him for something, I forgot what he said. What are you and Antonio doing?"

I was going to respond until the door opened and Chase was at the other end of it.

"You got that work bro?" Antonio said slapping him up.

"Yeah, you just did a drill huh?" He said shaking his head.

"Are yawl two serious?"

They both just looked at me,

"I thought your grandma called you over to her house. I guess Kylah don't know that you're here. Does she know anything? Is it a secret?"

I really was just asking, but I guess Chase took it as a threat. He got in my face and made me back into the door.

"If you tell her I swear to G-."

Antonio had one hand on his gun and the other on Chases' arm, pulling him back.

"Yo are you dumb? Don't ever step to my girl. You like a brother to me but I killed a lot of people's brothers, remember that."

Chase was shocked,

"Just make sure she doesn't say anything man, I don't know how Kylah would react and I love her too much."

Antonio looked him up and down and pushed him to the side. He grabbed my hand and we made are way back to Curry's room. We walked into the room and I made eye contact with Slim immediately. I quickly looked away and followed Antonio up to Curry's desk. He still looked fresh with all his chains and his security detail posted around him.

"Is it done? Is it clean?"

"Yeah, I snapped."

"Damn Skinner. You sure are like a son I wish I had. So check this out, it probably won't be that much time until your next one, as in, a couple days until you got to hit Kevin."

"Kevin?"

Antonio stepped back a little bit and his face was pale.

"Is that a problem Skinner?"

I grabbed Antonio's hand and he squeezed it.

"Kevin, he taught me everything, he's the most loyal person I know. Can't you put somebody else on the job?"

Curry laughed and summoned one of his boys up to the desk. Antonio pushed me back and nodded his head for Slim to grab me. I knew whatever was about to happen must've been bad for him to let Slim near me. I saw Antonio stand up straight and put his arms behind his back. Curry's security put a gun on the desk with the barrel facing Antonio. I started to walk towards him when slim grabbed me and pulled me back, covering my mouth. I watched as the security man punched Antonio repeatedly. Tears streamed down my face.

"IS HANDLING KEVIN GOING TO BE A PROBLEM?"

The man said, holding Antonio's face up.

"Yes!" He said without breaking. The man threw him onto the ground, Antonio was about to stand up when the man grabbed the gun and pointed it at Antonio. The man looked back at Curry, he pointed in my direction and the man redirected the gun to me.

"No, please Curry please, come on don't make me do this."

I was Antonio's weakness…Again. Curry pulled out a stack of money from his desk and had the security guy from the other side of him put it in a black bag along with a file.

"I trust this bag of money," Curry said calling back the guard with his gun on me "and me deciding to let home girl live is more than enough leverage for you to get this job done. When I say you, I mean nobody else, he'll kill anybody else I send. You better get this done quick. You got two weeks to fight your demons' boy."

He said ordering both guards to lift him up. Slim let me go and I ran to Antonio. Curry started laughing,

"Oh, what I'd do for love. Go on now son, before I remember that you're not really my son."

Antonio grabbed the bag of money and spit blood from his mouth onto the floor in front of the guard. He grabbed my hand and walked out the room. Chase came up to him and apologized again. He got in the car with us and we dropped him back off with Kylah. She texted me moments after saying he was back, I felt so bad knowing that not only did I know where he was, but I dropped him off to her without her knowing...

CHAPTER 11

We sat there for a moment before he pulled off. I could see he was trying to get his thoughts together.

"Baby?"

I said wiping the blood from his lip.

"I'm fine, don't even worry about it."

It was 11:15, he didn't seem like he wanted to be bothered, but we went to "Cravings" a restaurant that was open all night. We usually sit on opposite sides of the booth but this time he pulled me next to him.

"Antonio?"

I touched his face lightly, but he still jumped back.

"I'm sorry."

I said watching him wipe the blood from his lip. He looked at me with sad eyes, I could tell he was trying to hide it.

"What do you want to eat babe?"

I looked at the menu, trying not to ask him if he was ok, disregarding how much pain I knew he was in.

"Um, just wings and fries."

Antonio didn't bother to look at the menu, and I couldn't ignore his pain anymore.

"Do you want to talk about what happened? Tell me who Kevin is?"

Before he could get a word out, the waitress greeted us. We ordered two lemon waters, I got wings with fries and Antonio got a burger. The waiter left, Antonio hesitated, but began to speak.

"Kevin is like a brother. I've known him since I was 12. He's a few years older than me, so I'll say he was 15 or 16. He used to live down the street from me during that time, he looked over me when the other boys on the street and at school would pick on me. When he noticed I started to look up to him, he started bringing me to Curry. I knew he was one of the up and coming thugs, but I always thought he just sold drugs or something along those lines. The summer of last year he called me down to his house and said we were going on a trip. We got in his car and drove about 45 minutes out of town to an old house in the back woods. When we walked in, the man who opened the door began to run automatically. Kevin shot him in the leg. I didn't even flinch, I don't know if it was because I was in shock, or if it really just didn't bother me at all. He told me to look inside of everything, searching for money that he owed Curry. I found it inside of the couch. I remember watching the man plead for his life. Kevin let me do the honors. He was so proud of me. This was during the time my dad was cheating on my mom and it seemed like everyone around me was a snake, except him."

The waiter brought us our drinks and told us our food would be out shortly, he took a big gulp and continued.

"He took me under his wing and kept me there, he was one of Curry's favorites that's how I got in so good with him. There always comes a day where the student feels like they don't need the teacher. For Kevin, that day came at the end of last year, and he got kicked out. I decided to stay with Curry. Kevin was going to build his hood from the ground up, but by then I was making too much money and I didn't want to risk going back to the bottom of the food chain. So I betrayed him, I turned my back on him. I'd been hearing rumors that Kevin was sending for Curry's head, I guess he heard that too, so he put me on the job. Not only does Kevin have the skills to take down everyone in that house at once, but if Curry was to send somebody else to tail him, go to his door or even step foot in his hood, he would know something was up. But I can't kill him…I mean, I have to, but it'll haunt me."

After hearing Antonio's story about Kevin, I felt like I understood him way better.

"I never thought something like that would be the cause for everything that goes on now, I can't believe your dad was cheating on your mom. I'm sorry this happened to you at such a young age."

I said stroking his hand gently.

"I don't mind what you do on your spare time, I just needed a little time to adjust. Like you said, I'm a rider. I'm not going anywhere."

I leaned my head on his shoulder and allowed myself to completely forget about the nightmare. He isn't a monster after all. The waiter brought out our food a few moments later, I was glad it wasn't too packed. I looked over at Antonio, I noticed he was having trouble chewing his food. He saw me staring at him through the corner of his eye. When he turned his head to look at me, I noticed his jaw was swollen,

"There's a cut inside of my mouth."

I kissed his jaw,

"I could nurse you back to health tonight."

I said leaning against him. Antonio smiled and we continued to eat our food in silence. The waiter came with the bill soon after we were finished, Antonio paid it and left the him a100-dollar tip. He grabbed my hand and walked out of the restaurant.

"So about the gun."

I said innocently, Antonio laughed.

"Maybe one day you can have it, but you don't need it now."

I stared at his jaw while he pulled out the driveway. I am his weakness. During the ride home, we had light conversation, I was just trying to ease his mind a bit.

"Can I come in for desert?" Antonio said with a smile.

"Not tonight, you have to go home and take care of your jaw, make sure you're back to normal for the party tomorrow. If you're good you can have a feast."

I kissed Antonio softly on the lips before I got out the car.

"Have a good night. I love you."

Antonio smiled,

"I love you too K."

I opened the door and waved back to Antonio to let him know he could pull off. Right after I closed and locked the door Kylah called.

"I hate Chase!"

"Why? What did he do?"

"When he was grabbing his charger out his coat, drugs fell out his pocket! Why would he keep something like this from me?"

I felt guilty because I knew what was going on.

"I don't know why he would do that; he was probably going to tell you. He doesn't seem like the type of person that can keep a secret forever. Where is he now?"

"I don't know where he went, he stormed off after we started arguing. Now that I think about it, he probably lied to me about going to his grandmothers' house."

"Just try to talk to him about it." I said walking up to my room. "Maybe he had a good reason for keeping it from you."

"I don't know what to think about Chase or this situation." Kylah said raising her voice. "Whatever, I have a headache, I'm going to bed. Good night."

It seemed like everything was falling apart right before the party. I really hoped they make up by then. I decided against calling Antonio because I figured he needed his space. It was pushing 1:00 so I just got in the shower to make myself tired. It worked. After I got out and got some pajamas on I fell asleep almost immediately. I slipped into a dream rather quickly as well.

It started off with me seeing Cassie, I mean, 5-year-old me sleep. I watched the sun come up and my mother appeared in next to the bed.

"Rise and shine buttercup."

I heard her say softly, rubbing my head. I woke up and was immediately happy to see her. I jumped into her arms and she carried me out the room. I shifted through the house along with them. She brought me down to the kitchen and I saw my father cooking breakfast, I jumped from my mother's arms into his.

"Papa!"

I heard myself screech. I began to cry, I was watching all of this happen, like it wasn't me as a little girl.

Next thing I know I was in the backseat of the car, sitting next to my child self. My dad pulled off and I looked around, I noticed a car following closely behind us.

"Martin!" I screamed on the top of my lungs, "Dad! Turn around, please! Look!"

My plead fell on deaf ears. I saw the first rain drop fall from the sky and onto the window. I knew exactly what this dream was, I tried to wake myself but I couldn't. All of a sudden it started pouring and my child-self began to sing.

"I'm a little teapot short and stout. Here is my handle, here is my spout!"

I was so happy as a child. My mother sang along with me. My heart started racing once they turned on to the road that was in the report. I looked back and Martin was still following us. I grabbed my child-self's hand and closed my eyes, trying to relax and wake myself up. Martin's car began to speed up, I heard my mother scream.

"Carson!"

My child self's voice fell flat. Martin smashed into the side of the car. My mother's head snapped back to see if my child self was ok. I looked so scared and confused. My father struggled to get control of the car. Martin swerved his own car, smashing into ours repeatedly. We flew through the railing, all of a sudden I was outside of the car, watching everything happen. I heard my mother scream out for my father, I assumed he was the first to die. I dropped down to my knees. I watched as Martin got out of the car swiftly. He pulled my child self out of the car and ran back to his, I was screaming and kicking. He threw me in the back seat and returned over to the car with a bottle of gasoline and a match.

"Stop!"

I screamed running after him, I tried my hardest to hit him and push him away, but I kept going through him, and he couldn't hear me. I watched as the car went up in flames and the rain began to slow down, and eventually it went down to a light mist. I got inside the car with my younger self and watched myself scream and bang on the window.

"Mama! Papa!"

I screamed as I watched my face while my childhood got taken away. Martin came back to the car, went to the trunk, came back and put a cloth to my face. My younger self passed out instantly. I sat in the back seat with myself silently. Martin was so calm, he just continued on driving like he didn't just kill two people and steal a child…He stole me.

We drove for a while until we pulled into a junk yard. I saw my uncle waiting for Martin.

"Here she is. My little girl, Kori."

He said pulling me out the car and handing my limp body to my uncle.

"I got everything ready."

He walked back to the car and adjusted his mirror. We made eye contact, I wasn't worried because I thought he couldn't see me, but he did.

"Who the hell are you!"

He said. I got out the car and began to run as fast as I could, I tripped over a tire and Martin stood over me. He pulled out a gun and I heard a beeping noise over and over again. He pulled the trigger and I shot out of my sleep, my alarm was going off and it was time for school. I decided to just get dressed instead of showering, not only because I showered a few hours ago, but because I had flash backs of my dream when I turned the water on. I looked out of my window and saw Martin's car. He's officially dead to me. I checked my phone for messages but there were none.

I threw my hair into a pony tail and put on leggings and a baggy T-shirt. I didn't want anybody that was going to be at the party to see me look even halfway presentable, just so I could blow them away later. I always got away with doing my homework at school, but I happened to have a lot today. It was only 7, but I snuck past Martin's room, grabbed a granola bar and began to walk to school. While I walked I saw Antonio pull up behind me.

"You look good girl. You need a ride?"

"That's the line you're going with?" I said walking slowly next to the car. "You do look good though."

Antonio stopped the car and got out.

"Do a little twirl ma."

I laughed and spun around. I could feel Antonio studying every inch of my body, even though I was in street clothes.

"Whew, I was waiting for the right girl to give this to, who knew it would be a sexy girl walking down the street." Antonio pulled out a little box from his jacket and my heart started racing.

"You didn't!"

I said pushing him. He opened the box, inside was a beautiful gold diamond ring in molded into a shape of a heart.

"This must've cost a fortune!"

"Kori, you're talking like I didn't just get a duffel bag full of money yesterday." He said taking the ring out of the holder. "Put it on, I want to make sure it fits."

"It's perfect baby!"

I said putting my hand out to show him. He kissed me, put the box inside my bag and opened my door. We got in the car and he pulled off

"So, what are you going to do about Kevin?"

"I'm going to give him 5grand, tell him to disappear, take one of the chains he had from way back in the day to show Curry, that'll be it."

"But, what if he doesn't want to disappear?"

I said, hoping he didn't get upset that I was asking.

"Then I'm going to kill him."

I didn't respond, I knew Antonio was trying to be strong, like it wouldn't bother him to kill Kevin. I watched the other cars roll by, and the "nerds" walk through the school parking lot.

"Why you going to school so early anyways?"

"Just a lot of homework I won't have time to do during my study hall."

He shook his head and pulled into the parking lot, I noticed we both had on grey pants, a white T-shirt, sneakers and gold jewelry. I smiled at the unplanned matching and kissed him repeatedly, even though I would see him later when school actually started. We sat in the car for a while,

"You ready for the party baby?"

"Yeah, I just hope Kylah and Chase make up before the last bell. He dropped some drugs out of his pocket last night and they got in a huge fight."

Antonio shook his head. He couldn't hide the disgust on his face.

"You still mad at him huh?"

"You thought me pulling the gun out on slim was bad? If I would've took the gun out of my pocket I would've shot Chase, you know why I didn't? Not because I didn't want to, but because the blood would've gotten on you."

"Antonio."

I said concerned. He started laughing hysterically.

"I'm a killer. I can't have feelings. Why am I having nightmares about killing some dude that used to take me to the ice cream truck? Why is some girl my weakness?"

Some girl? I thought to myself. I went to respond, but I couldn't, he was clearly hurting and I refused to hear something that would hurt my feelings. I got out of the car and slammed the door. I quickly slapped the tears from my face and stood up straight. When I started to walk away I could hear Antonio yell my name, and say he was sorry. He didn't try to chase me down, so I didn't believe him, I guess he just didn't expect to let that come out of his mouth.

CHAPTER 11

When I got into school I threw myself into my work, I blocked out all my thoughts. At least I tried to. I looked up when I saw a group of kids walking towards the side door, I caught a glimpse of my parents. I blinked, the next thing I knew they were gone. All of a sudden my phone started ringing off the hook with messages from Martin, Antonio and Kylah.

Martin text me asking me where I was and where I've been. Antonio pleaded for forgiveness and Kylah whined about Chase. I couldn't even think, about anything. I turned my phone off and watched the clock. I noticed a teacher walking back and forth, and we continued to make eye contact.

"Can I help you?"

I said to her with an attitude. I watched her walk slowly up to me.

"You know a watched pot never boils."

"Excuse me?"

She laughed.

"If you keep staring at that clock, the time will drag on forever."

I ignored her and put my eyes back to the clock.

"You look sad. Do you want to tell me what's wrong?"

She pulled up a chair next to me. I looked at her face and I couldn't help but make connections to my mother. I figured it was because I was tired and thinking about her, so I just shrugged it off.

"You don't really care, and you really don't know me. I know when you look at me you're thinking that I'm about to be sad over one of these high school boys screwing my best friend and my CEO father shutting me out of his life. I'm sorry miss but you're barking up the wrong tree."

"What's your name?"

"Kori, Kori Tucker."

I leaned back in my chair so I can make myself seem like a rebel child that doesn't care. I watched her write something down on a notepad she pulled out of her pocket. I quickly looked back to the clock when I noticed that she stopped writing.

"Well Kori, call me when you're ready to talk."

She winked at me and walked into the crowd of kids getting ready for the bell to ring. I don't know why she bothered me so much. I mean it would be relaxing to talk to someone completely outside of everything I was going through.

The bell rung and I swung my bag over my shoulder and walked slowly to my homeroom instead of going to my locker. I was the first one there so I just sat there, drawing pictures in my notebook. Antonio walked in and I rolled my eyes, I refused to look at him.

"Baby, look at me."

He grabbed my hands, when I refused to budge, he got down on his knees.

"Please baby, I'm so sorry."

People were starting to gather around the door and come inside the room.

"Get up, you're embarrassing yourself."

"Fuck everybody in here. You know nobody will say anything about me or you."

I rolled my eyes and tried to pull him up but he wouldn't move. I looked him in his eyes.

"Ok Antonio!" I said kissing him over and over. "See, I forgive you, you can get up now."

My teacher came in and the rest of the class followed. He got up and grabbed my arm.

"I need to borrow her Miss."

He said pulling me out of the class before she could say anything. The halls emptied quicker than usual. I guess all the popular people who stayed in the hallway just wanted this day to go by quicker. Antonio pulled me into the girls' bathroom that was in the back hall without cameras. He pulled the string of my sweatpants and untied my bow. I smacked him and he pushed me up against the wall. He held me down with one arm and shoved the other hand down my pants. I continued to struggle and scratch up his arm. He slipped his middle finger inside me and I began to feel weak, like I was melting.

"St-Stop."

The word felt like it was being dragged out of my mouth.

"You stop!"

He slipped in another finger and began to move faster. He held me up as I began to slip down the wall.

"Damn…" I said trying to find the strength to actually fight back. "I hate you."

"I know." Antonio took his hand back and turned me around.

"No!" I yelled, holding my arm out behind me.

"No?" Antonio said shocked. "Whatever K."

He continued, pulling down my pants, doing the same with his. He pushed inside of me and pulled my hair.

"I didn't mean it." He said over and over again. "I love you Kori."

I was mad that it felt good. I was hurt because of what he said. I didn't respond. He went in deeper and harder with every stroke. My hair was pulled completely out of the ponytail so he had no choice but to twist it in his hands. I let out a loud moan.He covered my mouth with his other hand. He had complete control over me. I got weaker with every stroke of his wet warm tongue on my neck. Every suction and every bite. I got weaker with every slow stroke he forced deep inside me. He let me finish and pulled up his pants, got right on his knees and made me finish again…and again.

"Stop being mad."

"I can't believe you just did that." I said fixing my hair. "I can't believe you said that… Some girl Antonio? Really? I see now that you know exactly how to hurt me."

"Baby, you know I-."

I cut him off before he could apologize again.

"I don't want to hear it. You did mean it. It's ok. I know you're hurt, I know I'm your weakness, I know you never loved before. My dad hit me when he felt upset and my uncle was only there to wipe my tears, shut the door and go on to being secretive with him. So, this is the first time I've truly loved too."

Antonio flinched when I mentioned my dad hitting me.

"I will kill him, you know, if you want me to. Brutally." He added, "Or, just beat him an inch from the end of his life."

"No, I'm good. I basically skipped first period so, thank you."

I began to walk towards the door and Antonio grabbed my arm and pushed me back up against the wall.

"Skip the rest of it."

"I hate you!" I said, I felt tears stream down my face. I couldn't keep it together. I couldn't keep acting like I was a rock.

"There we go, there's Kori. I knew you cared. Why you acting like you weren't hurt? Baby I'm so sorry, I directed my anger and sadness towards the wrong person. I promise you, you aren't just some girl, You're Kori Rivet, my wife. My rider, my first love, gone be my baby moms, cause the way you be feeling, I mean damn."

I rolled my eyes and he wiped the tears from them.

"Please bae, I didn't mean to make you cry. Forgive me?"

"I forgive you, can I go to class now?"

Antonio nodded and kissed me on the cheek, I walked slowly back to class. As soon as I got to the room, the bell rung. Since I had to go in to grab my bag, I gave my teacher the homework before she gave me a detention. Apparently nobody but me did it so I got a free pass. I really hated being popular sometimes, I could never keep to myself, everybody was watching me, seeing what I was going to do next. Then there were the other popular people that automatically assumed I wanted to be their friend. I wouldn't trade it for the world though, it definitely had perks. Who doesn't want people to move out of their way when they walk in the halls, or have people mark the day you actually talk to them in their calendar.

I caught a glimpse of the lady from the cafeteria this morning, I've never seen her before, and I get the feeling I won't be able to stop seeing her. I saw Chase and I called him over.

"Have you seen Kylah?"

"Yeah, I saw her duck behind somebody earlier, trying to avoid me."

He walked away with his head down, I didn't know if I felt bad for him or not. I turned my phone back on to text Kylah to see where she was because I had a substitute for my next class and I knew she never went to second period. I ran into her in the hall as she was responding to me.

"Can you stop?"

I said, bumping her.

"No. I'm mad at him and I'm going to stay mad!"

"What about the party?"

She rolled her eyes,

"I'll still go and make him look good, I'll try not to show my disgust in front of the team and their groupies."

I felt a wave of relief, I did not want to go alone. We walked through all floors, everybody went into class today. We just continued to be bored and walk around, until we saw Haley and her posy coming our way. I sighed, I did not have time for this.

"Coming to the party tonight?" Haley said, walking way too close to me.

"Girl you better back up and mind your business." Kylah said, trying to push in front of me. Haley laughed.

"I was talking to Kori, side kick."

"Yeah, I'll be at the party. I just hope you don't have any secrets that'll be exposed after too many drinks." I winked and nodded at Kylah to come on.

"What was that supposed to mean? You had her stuck."

"You can't say anything." I said, pulling Kylah into a corner. "She drunk herself into a miscarriage, Antonio didn't even know she was pregnant, that's why they broke up."

Kylah was shocked, she just shook her head and continued to walk. We just sat on the stairs until the bell rung, it just happened to be near the classes Chase and Antonio came out of. I pushed Kylah into Chase and forced them to make up, I knew she couldn't stay mad. Antonio picked me up and continued walking down the hall.

"Can you put me down, everybody is staring."

"Everybody would be staring regardless."

I smacked my teeth and let him carry me. We saw one of the basketball groupies, Antonio seemed like he was going out of his way to ignore her.

"Yo, Toni, remember last year? How about a repeat?"

Antonio put me down.

"Nasty bitch don't ever say anything to me when I'm with my girl. You want to get a train ran on you again? By how many of us this time?"

"Don't call me that! You're so rude."

I was shocked by this entire situation. She walked around him, and came up to me.

"He's good right?"

I spit in her face.

"Are they all good hoe?"

We both laughed at her, she ran down the hall crying. A few moments later, my name was being called over the loud speaker. When I walked in I saw the lady from this morning.

"I got this one."

She said to the principal. I rolled my eyes, I would rather be suspended than have to have a counseling session with her. She had an undeniable similarity to my mother. We walked for a few minutes down to her office. I've never noticed it before. I walked in and helped myself to a seat.

"So, you're spitting on people and calling them whores?"

"Yep, pretty much."

She shuffled through some files and pulled out on with my name on it.

"So, you transferred here from a private school, never been suspended, have been on the honor roll all your life and now you're here. Still on the honor roll, dating the most popular boy in school, Antonio Rivet." She shuffled through more files and pulled out his. He himself has been in a public school all his life, comes from a very wealthy family and has been on the honor roll as well. He has a bit of a record when it comes to suspensions though. Hmm. So Kori, you going to tell me what's up?"

"Who are you?" I said pulling my chair closer to her desk.

"I'm a psychiatrist."

I figured that this was my chance, I was scared, but she doesn't have to know the situation I bring up is about me.

"Say, hypothetically, there was a girl who just recently found out she went through a traumatic experience when she was younger. And say this girl, um I don't know, found out somebody knew her before this tragedy happened and teamed up with her to figure out all the pieces of the puzzle. Ok, now say this girl can't stop thinking about the experience. She sees or hears things that make her have flashbacks of the past and she has nightmares about it. Say this girl feels intense whenever she's in a car, or now whenever she sees rain or when the shower comes on, or woman with black hair and men with a suit. What would that be?"

She cleared her throat,

"I would say, hypothetically, that girl has PTSD."

"A mental disorder?"

"Yes, PTSD is a mental disorder caused by a traumatic event that you witness or went through, such as yourself. It involves flashbacks, nightmares and/or anxiety."

I guess she was right, that did sound like me…Exactly like me actually.

"I said a girl, I said hypothetically."

"Yes of course. Sorry for the confusion. Anyways, tell that girl that I'm here if she ever needs to talk about something non-hypothetical, and that it's the only way she'll begin to recover. Also, let her know that admitting she has a problem, is the best way to begin the process of solving it. Now, if you would please keep the spit inside your mouth and refrain from calling anybody names, I will keep in school suspension off the table, got it Ms. Tucker?"

I agreed, gathered my things and left. I went from class to class, handing in all my work and completing all class assignments. Kylah was doing the same because we barely spoke to each other in English. We got to hang out and talk about the party in Study hall and gym. I knew it would be awkward since Antonio already agreed to take Kylah and I to my house, and take Chase to the athlete house to get ready for the party. I was scared leaving Chase alone with Antonio, knowing he had no issues killing him, but I knew he wouldn't.

CHAPTER 12

By the time the bell rung and we all met up after we went to our lockers Kylah and Chase seemed to be made up. I could tell Kylah was trying to act like she wasn't upset because she didn't want to be anymore. All four of us walking down the hallway together caught more attention than a 3 headed dragon would've, but we all looked straight ahead and ignored it. There was more tension than a little bit that I could feel, not only because of Chase and Kylah, but Chase and Antonio too. Antonio blasted a song by Free man, a well-known rapper. Antonio rapped along

"And that man must be a fool, I'm not scared to grab a tool. You could be my brother and yeah we might've been cool. You cross me? I double cross you!"

I punched him in the arm and took his phone off the aux cord.

"Isn't that right Chase?" Antonio said staring at him through the rear view mirror. Chase started to squirm in his seat.

"You're so mean." I said, rolling my eyes.

We pulled up to the house, I kissed Antonio goodbye and Kylah kissed Chase. When he got up to get in the front seat, Antonio locked the door and yelled at him to stay in the back, he smacked his teeth, and got back in the car. After Antonio pulled off, me and Kylah went in the house, my dad was there but he was cooped up inside of his room. We got into mine and I started to undress.

"What's that about?" Kylah said, pulling clothes out of her tote bag.

"I don't know, something petty. I know you didn't completely forgive Chase, you actually should instead of just acting like it."

"If I act like it long enough, I actually will forgive him."

I shrugged my shoulders and got my clothes and jewelry together.

"I'm about to hop in the shower."

I said pinning my hair up and putting on a robe. When I walked into the bathroom I stared at the knob for at least 5 minutes before I got the courage to turn it on. After I did, I washed up 3 times as quickly as I could and tried my hardest not to think. When I got back to my room Kylah was dressed and looked stunning.

"Damn best friend." I said, smacking her butt.

"Girl, you know we got to show out." She said laughing. "Curl my hair after you get dressed, I'll do yours."

I put on the dress Antonio got me with his number on it, fish net stockings and his chain, another gold necklace, a gold watch, big hoop earrings and nude lip stick. I got a text from Antonio saying the hummer limo was set and they would be to pick us up in 30 minutes. We used that time to do each other's hair and make a quick to-go bag with deodorant, lotion, perfume, hair pins and a few other necessities inside. We heard a honk outside, so we ran out the door. When Antonio and Chase stepped out the limo, me and Kyla's jaw dropped. They both had on a black and white dry-fit shirt with their numbers on it and a suit bottom, jacket and bow tie.

We all said "Damn baby." At the same time. Antonio opened the door for Kylah and I, when we got in, the limo was even bigger than it looked on the outside. We all had a ball on our way there, so I knew the party would be even better.

When we got there, it was already lit. There was music, dancing, drugs, drinking games and teenagers making out and laughing. From the moment we walked in, Chase and Antonio got love from everybody from all different schools and parts of town. The guys slapped them up and did basketball chants, and of course girls were swarming around them asking for hugs and to take pictures. A dancing song came on and Antonio pulled me closer to say something, I couldn't hear him so he pulled me onto the dance floor. I was nervous because I never danced on him to music like this, and definitely not in front of people. I looked over to find Kylah, when she saw me she mouthed the words "Dance bestie!" and gave me a thumbs up. Antonio pressed me onto his body, I was nervous, but I began to my hips slowly.

"Come on bae, I know you can do better than that." Antonio said, grabbing me harder and pressing me against him. I decided to let loose and stop acting so uncomfortable. I started to go faster, moving my butt and hips in a circle. I could feel Antonio getting excited. People started to stare and scream.

"Get it Toni!"

I could hear girls whispering.

"Who is that?"

Kylah walked up to them. "That's his girlfriend. Get it best friend! You're killing it."

Antonio started to move with me, by then he was on 10. Right before things got more intense, the song stopped. We strolled off the dance floor and walked up to Chase and Kylah.

"Best friend I didn't know you could dance like that. Let me find out."

I just laughed.

"Girl I'm naturally talented."

Antonio grabbed my butt.

"Mm, you sure are."

He roughly kissed me on the lips. All of a sudden I felt pressure on my jaw.

"Did someone just hit me?"

I said out loud to myself. I looked around and saw Kylah pushing Haley to the ground.

"Fucking side kick tell your partner in crime to stop running her mouth. She thinks she's so funny because Antonio pumped her little ass up."

Antonio grabbed my arm and held me back.

"Girl wasn't nobody thinking about you! Don't ever put your fucking hands on me."

"We just got here and you're already starting shit!"

Kylah added as Haley stood up and squared up with her.Kylah was too quick, she hit her with combos and jabs, all Haley could do was grab her hair and drag her to the ground. I jumped in and began to punch her in the face and back of the head until she let go. Haley wildly swung and got a cheap shot to my nose. Antonio pushed Haley, knocking her down as Chase helped Kylah up.

I ran to the bathroom and wet some paper towels to wipe the blood from my face. I grabbed another one and pressed it to my nose, hoping the bleeding would stop. I heard a bunch of commotion coming from the street, so I ran outside. I couldn'tfind Kylah, Antonio or Chase. I continued to spin in circles and push through the crowd looking for them. When I turned towards the street I saw Martin, just standing there. I felt a few rain drops hit my skin and everybody ran back inside, but I was stuck, staring at Martin. I saw a car pull up to the red light, there was a little girl in the back seat crying. My body began to feel heavy and my heart started to beat out of my chest. When I looked back over to Martin, he was gone and the car pulled off. The rain picked up and all of a sudden Antonio swept me off my feet and brought me inside.

"You alright baby? Haley ran out, I don't want her to ruin your fun."

"I'm good bae, come on, let's party."

I ran over to Kylah to make sure she was alright, but she was already taking shots with some girls from Grant high, so I joined them. I threw a few back and laughed with the girls. I noticed that I hadn't seen Antonio for a while, I looked around and saw him standing in the corner with two guys behind him. He was talking to somebody I saw walk in the door, he was really popular, but was unfamiliar to me. I could tell he belonged amongst the older guys that were there. Antonio seemed tense and he was gripping the gun in his pants. I cautiously walked over there and grabbed his hand. Antonio snatched away from me.

"Antonio?"

I said confused.

"Oh, this yo shorty?" The unfamiliar man looked me up and down.

"Nah."

Antonio said, pushing me away. I was so confused.

"Baby, what are you-."

I started to say, but Antonio cut me off

"Get out of here groupie, find somebody else to bother."

The man laughed.

"It's a damn shame."

The boys behind Antonio lifted me up and carried me back over to Kylah. I felt sick.

"I need to go."

I said to Kylah as I ran out of the party. I got into the limo and took a long deep breath. The chauffeur asked me if I was alright, I closed the partition and began to cry non-stop. Kylah came into the limo soon after.

"Best friend what happened?"

I couldn't keep myself together long enough to tell her what happened. I heard her call Chase and he came out too.

"We're going to take you home, ok?"

I shook my head and laid on her lap. I couldn't think, I felt like my mind was in a foggy maze with no way out. When we got to my house Chase carried me to the door. I slowly walked up to my room, I heard Martin talking to me but I didn't even try to respond. I stripped down to my underwear, I was still drunk so I practically passed out when my head hit the pillow. Around 4 my phone started ringing off the hook with calls from Antonio, I turned my phone off and went back to sleep.

CHAPTER 13

It was 9am when I was rudely awakenedby Antonio, shaking me until I opened my eyes.

"Get out!" I said punching and kicking him.

"Baby."

"Stop touching me! Stop calling me baby! I'm a groupie remember? I thought I was a rider, your wife and all that. I guess it's different when you're around certain people. You should go."

Antonio pinned me down and sighed.

"I said that to protect you."

"How is hurting my feelings for the second time today protecting me! You didn't even come look for me after I ran out. I don't feel like talking. I have a hangover."

I said struggling to break free from his grip.

"Kevin was the one I was talking to at the party. The one who asked if you were my girl. Somebody put word in his ear that Curry sent out one of the vets to off him. He came to me talking about it, but I could tell he already had an idea that it was me even though he didn't say it. Like I said, he taught me everything, which means this man is ruthless, if he knew you were my girl he would kill you and send your head to my door step with a video of him doing it. Want to know how I know? Because I held the camera once." He let go of me after I calmed down and continued. "I won't be there to protect you all the time, so I had to act like I didn't care about you. I'm so sorry baby.

My heart raced as I looked at him.

"I understand. Babe I was so scared and hurt. I thought you didn't want anything to do with me anymore."

"That will never happen. Plus, I put my hands on a whole female for you, if that's not love I don't know what is."

He said laughing and running his fingers through my hair.

"Baby, everybody knows we're a couple, he's bound to find out sooner or later, my guess is sooner. What are you going to do when he does?"

"I hate to say, but me offering him money to leave is out the window now. The way he stepped to me yesterday, I know I have to kill him."

My hangover got the best of me at the wrong time. I leaned over the bed and grabbed my trash can. Antonio grabbed my hair as I threw up.

"You're such a light weight."

He said laughing and patting my back.

"I know this may sound crazy, but you need to take another shot to level you out. I'm about to run and get you a little something, some water, Gatorade, soup and a bunch of snacks. Alright baby?"

I shook my head as he tucked me back into bed. While he was gone I contemplated never drinking again. I heard Martin shuffling around down stairs, I figured drinking is exactly what he was doing. He burst into my room a few moments later.

"I was ta-talking to y-you last night."

He said, swinging from the door knob. I covered my face with the blankets and gripped it tight, I knew what was about to happen.

"Don't you dare hide from me Macey!"

"Who's Macey! I'm your daughter! Daddy it's me, Kori!"

I kicked and screamed as he dragged me off the bed.

"Why won't you stay dead!"

He punched and kicked me, throwing me against the wall and dressers. I tried to scream, but that did no good.

"Babe, I already had some stuff in the car that can hold you o-."

Antonio dropped the things he had in his hand.

"Baby! Help me."

My dad stopped hitting me and turned around. Antonio got unusually calm,

"Call the police, tell them we need an ambulance. NOW!"

I ran out of the door with blood dripping from my face, it hurt to breathe. I felt like my ribs were cracked. All I heard upstairs were cries from

Martin. Apologizing to me and begging for his life. I went back into my room but I stopped in the door way. Antonio looked like a different person, there was anger all over his face. Martin wheezed on the ground, Antonio's knuckles were bleeding. I watched him spit on Martin repeatedly. He kept punching him, Martin's body was limp. Antonio put his hands around his neck, that's when I knew I had to stop him.

"Baby! Baby stop it. Please!"

He got up from on top of him, like he as snapping back into reality. He quickly went into the bathroom and washed the blood from his face and hands. I became weak, every inch of me was in pain. I heard 3 ambulances and cop cars pull around the block. Antonio picked me up and walked me down the stairs and outside to the ambulance.

"Make sure she's alright, her dad put his hands on her. He's upstairs to the right, he'll need a stretcher though."

I didn't want to let go of his hand, but they put me into the ambulance and drove me to the hospital, I didn't get to see Martin be dragged out, I'm afraid that he might be dead. Antonio followed closely behind us and stayed with me the entire time. I had a few bruised ribs and a bit of a concussion, a busted lip and a knot swelling from my cheek. Antonio helped me cover as much of my face with makeup as I could. I was just glad the hospital gave me pain pills that made me feel like I was on Cloud 9. I knew I needed to call my uncle…Aaron for my insurance, I was hoping that this was their slip up, but apparently not, I was discharged.

"What the hell happened!"

I rolled my eyes and just let Aaron yell. I knew he worked for some part of the government or something that would help finalize my kidnapping and make me seem like Martin's daughter. I ignored him and ran into Antonio's arms.

"Are you ok?"

He said kissing me all over.

"I love you, I love you so much. Come on, we're going to my house."

He carried me to the car and laid me down in the backseat, I could see him and Aaron arguing, but he saw what he did to Martin. They might've come to some agreement. All I knew was I was going home with Antonio. I text Angela while we were in the car and told her that this would be her only chance to break into the room and find everything that she needed, I knew Aaron would stay at the hospital.

The only people home were Antonio's dad and little sister, he told him the situation and took me upstairs. I could tell the stand offish attitude Antonio had towards him, and now I understood why. We laid together for hours watching movies and eating unhealthy foods that we would regret later. I knew he was skipping practice for me, but I knew there wouldn't be consequences based on the situation.

"So baby, I've had this for a little bit and after that thing with Kevin and your dad today, I'm going to give you this gun."

He pulled out a leopard print and gold pistol from under his bed.

"It's already bullets inside, let me know if you need more. Oh yeah, I got you a silencer to match mine."

"I don't know how to shoot a gun."

Antonio put it back in the case and told me to come on.

"Where are we going?"

I said as he put my shoes on and gave me another pain pill.

"To curry, I'm about to teach you, and I got some business to handle."

We drove over there. I was extremely tense but I tried to calm down. It was pretty empty for it to be 2pm. We walked straight back to Curry's room.

"Well look who it is. Batman and Robin. Come here girl."

Curry said, waving me over to him. I walked to his side slowly.

"You want to learn how to shoot?"

I shook my head and Antonio handed me the case with the gun. Curry told me to put it on the desk, he put the silencer on for me.

"How you gone-."

Antonio started to say, but Curry put his hand up and he stopped talking. He whispered to the two men behind him and they left the room. He put the gun in my hand and got up. This was the first time I saw him stand. He was at least 6'6, that made him even more scary. He grabbed my arms and showed me how to aim the gun. The two men burst into the door carrying a struggling man, he was barely 20.

"Here we go!" Curry said laughing. "Hold the gun steady Robin. You see, this boy right here has been really bad. He stole from me. Can you believe that?"

My body tensed and I looked over to Antonio, he was just watching. I could tell that Curry had one eye on him.

"What...What do you want me to do?"

"Kill him."

The guy started to scream and squirm, the two men punched him in the face, I watched blood spill out of his mouth. He was quiet after that.

"I don't, I can't."

"You can, and you will. You got this animal for a boyfriend, I mean he is outstanding. I know he see's something in you, I see it too, come on Robyn."

Curry gave me a nudge on the shoulder.

"Come on Curry, when I said teach her how to shoot I meant give her a target sheet in the back, not a person. She's too good."

"Ok Skinner. You kill him."

Antonio pulled out his gun without hesitation. He looked the guy right in his face.

"Baby, I can do it."

His head snapped to the side. He dropped the gun and walked over to me.

"Do you know what you're asking to do?"

"Don't worry batman, she's got it. Go ahead baby."

The men threw him to the ground and pinned plastic to the wall.

"Baby, you don't have to do this. Curry, Kevin knows."

Curry pulled a gun out his desk and shot the guy five times in the chest. I watched his eye roll in the back of his head. I dropped the gun, I was stuck. His men cleaned him up and left the room. Curry had Antonio lock the door.

"Kevin stepped to me at a party last night saying he heard you had a hit out on him. He brought two of is guys with him, and he wasn't coming off as a friend. I'm thinking we have a rat."

Curry hit the table over and over again. I jumped and Antonio pulled me over to him.

"Kill him, kill him right now!"

Curry began to pull money from his desk and throw it onto the floor.

"Call whoever you have to call."

"I think we need to pull a holder. He knows who all the hits are, he'll be expecting them, waiting for them. Who's got heart? Once somebody takes him out, I'll take out his men, I promise I'll bring his head to you."

"Who?"

"What about Chase?"

I said, watching Curry pace back and forth.

"Take this money." He said picking up at least 2,000dollars off the floor. "Talk to Chase, talk to whoever you think can do this."

Antonio put the money in a rubber band and slid it in his pocket. Curry packed up my gun and gave it to me.

"Batman and Robin. Until next time."

We got into the car, Antonio hesitated to pull off.

"Were you seriously going to kill him? Are you kidding?"

I didn't respond. He drove off and told me to ask Kylah if I could come over because he was going to talk to some of the boys he had in his pocket. I checked my phone to see if Angela responded, she said she was inside. I asked Antonio to drop me off at home, he was a bit leery, but he dropped me off and told me he would get me later.

I walked into the house slowly.

"Angela?"

"Come look at this."

I heard her yell from the room upstairs. I ran as fast as I could to see what she was looking at.

"He stalked you, and your parents for two years. He stalked me and Kylah for two years. He wrote letters to Aaron, apparently they had a falling out after their parents died. He'd been writing about how he was so excited that he and his girlfriend were getting serious then, a few months later she was pregnant. Then, all of a sudden the letters stopped. This was in 1990."

I ran to my room to grab the death certificate and Macey's diary. I knew there had to be a connection between all the dates. *Why does November 12th sound so familiar to me?*

"See if you can find some pictures of Macey."

Angela shuffled through boxes.

"That's her. Martin had a picture of her on the table. Wait a second."

I ran back into my room and grabbed the necklace I had on for me and Antonio's first date…November 12th. I walked back into the room and picked up the picture off the floor.

"This is the same necklace. Martin told me this was my mother's before she died in 1990, the letters stopped right after her death. You said he'd been stalking me for two years? My family was killed in 1992."

I flipped through the pages of the diary, looking for the entry where she said she lost the baby.

"She lost the baby in August, the next entry she wrote was the end of

September, saying he was interested in other people's family now. This is all connected."

"Yeah, Martin began to reach out to Aaron when he and Macey got serious. Then he continued to try to reconnect when he thought Aaron would be an uncle soon." Angela said going through the letters. "It says here that Aaron came to see him after Macey lost the baby, that could've been when what they connected over."

Angela grabbed a tote bag and put the letter and photos and a few other things she found inside of it.

"I'm not going to push our luck, we need to get the room in order and lock the door back."

I helped her make it seem like we were never there. We had small talk while we were doing it. Like how the party was and how school was, we both tried to mask our fear for what we'd just uncovered. I couldn't help but continue to wonder who locked the door and why. I tried to brush off the fact that I very well could have PTSD or whatever the lady said. I wondered if Macey actually did overdose or why Aaron was so on top of the idea to kidnap me. I wondered if they'd always been crazy. I didn't understand why they chose me or found me. I needed answers that could only come from Martin or Aaron and I knew that once the truth did come out, I probably still would never get them. I guess I had to be ok with that...

CHAPTER 14

We finished just in time, right after Angela left Antonio text me and told me he was outside. When I got in the car I called Kylah, I hadn't heard from her all day. When she answered she sounded like she was dead. She said she had a bad hangover because she and Chase went back to the party after they dropped me off. I laughed and let her go back to sleep.

"So what are we about to do baby?"

I said, popping two more pain killers.

"I'm about to take you shopping."

"Ooh, what's my limit?"

Antonio began to laugh. He pulled out the purse I left at his house earlier and opened it, there was 3 stacks of 100's inside.

"That's your limit."

We had a ball cashing out at the mall. We had to take three trips back to the car because we couldn't carry the bags. We bought matching outfits. We both got a few pairs of sneakers, and a lot of new jewelry. I got a bunch of purses and sweat suits, Antonio got a few more suits and even got gold bottoms. We showered together when we got back to his house and dried off in the covers. His kisses seemed to work wonders, or maybe it was just the pain killers. I was glad we had the entire day to spend together tomorrow, that way we could just be lazy and sleep in.

We woke up to Antonio's mom knocking on the door saying she made breakfast. Antonio rolled over and started smiling.

"What are you so happy about?"

I said fixing my hair and putting on clothes.

"I fell asleep and woke up with the most beautiful girl in the world. Who wouldn't be smiling."

Antonio said as he pulled me closer to him. He kissed down my back and tugged at the bow on my underwear.

"Not so fast baby, your mom made us breakfast."

"Mm, please, it'll be really quick bae. Only thing you have to do is that little trick from last night."

I laughed and made him put on clothes so we could go downstairs for breakfast. When we got down there it smelt even better than it did while we were in Antonio's room. I walked into the kitchen and his little sister ran right up to me, she only wanted me to sit with her at the table. She talked my ear off but I loved it, she was so cute and smart. She took me to her room and let me help her pick out something to wear for her play date. I did her hair and made sure she looked super cute like she asked. After doing that I was completely sure I won over his parents. About an hour later they all left to go do different things, saying they wouldn't be back until later. Antonio looked at me like I had a halo over my head.

"You're great with her."

"I know right. I feel like she's my little girl."

Antonio picked me up and took me back up to his room and started to undress me without saying a word.

"What are you doing crazy?"

"I'm about to get you pregnant."

He said undressing himself after.

"Baby, are you serious?"

He kissed up and down the length of my body, biting the inside of my thighs, teasing me.

"Mm, I am so serious. Kori Tucker, I want you to have my baby."

"Ok. I will. You better give me a baby girl."

Antonio smiled and pushed inside me. We went rounds and ended up in almost every room in the house.

"Damn, I think you might've gave me twins or triplets the way we were going."

I looked over to see him sleeping. I giggle, pulled the cover over us and laid on his chest. I told him I loved him right before his heart beat put me to sleep. When we woke up it was around 6. Everybody was back home and a half hour later we got called down for dinner. This time his dad cooked, he threw down in the kitchen making stuffed chicken and vegetables. I knew that he stepped out on Antonio's mom, but she seemed genuinely happy with him. When we got back to his room Antonio started to play the game. I was bored so I started to fold his clothes and made a section for myself inside the walk in closet. When I was finished I laid back on the bed.

"Baby, would you ever cheat on me?"

Antonio smacked his teeth and paused the game.

"Don't ever ask me no dumb shit like that."

Antonio seemed extremely offended that I would even ask. He started to play the game again and pulled out my gun from the case. I studied it, took the bullets out and put them back in, aimed it, acted like I was shooting. I even started to count some money I found inside a box in Antonio's closet, I had to count by the band. I stopped when I got to the 100th one.

"What are you going to do with all this money?"

I said putting it all back into sections.

"I'm gone pay off some people to help me kill Kevin, spend it on you and eventually give our baby the world."

I smiled and rubbed my stomach, I couldn't wait to take the test and find out I actually was pregnant.

"You excited about your game tomorrow? First game of the play offs right?"

"Yeah, it's going to be a lot of people there to support us. You coming right?"

I shook my head and picked out my outfit for tomorrow to waste some time. Antonio played the game for three more hours until he turned on a movie and got into bed with me. We ended up falling asleep an hour later and didn't wake up until the alarm went off at 6:30. We both took turns in the bathroom and got dressed together, we functioned pretty well. The conversation was scarce but I think we were both just tired and the events from yesterday were kicking in. We both stepped out looking particularly good today, it could be because we just went shopping but we always had nice clothes. I had to use the makeup I got to cover the bruises and scratches on my face that rose over night.

On our way to school we stopped and got some breakfast and picked up Kylah and Chase. This was starting to be a routine. We all got to school right on time and immediately went our separate ways. Of course Kylah and I met up for the last three periods of the day, but it was just a boring day in general. It didn't get exciting until the end of the day when we stayed after waiting for the game to start with a few other girls whom boyfriends played basketball and some of the cheerleaders. The game finally began and it started to get intense around second quarter.

"Go baby!"

I screamed every time I saw Antonio score on someone, assist or block a shot. Everybody screamed for different people, of course the groupies around Kylah and I screamed for Chase and Antonio, trying to be funny, but we chose to ignore it. The game seemed to fly by and Chasity ended up winning 110-86 against LRP high. We watched the boys jump around and do their chants. Antonio scored 43 points tonight, I definitely had to take him out. I leaned over to talk to Kylah, I had to yell over the crowd.

"Yeah, I'm definitely going to take him out tonight."

Kylah smiled and made kissing noises. She acted like she wasn't head over heels for Chase. My phone started ringing, it was Antonio.

"Congratulations baby, you better be free because I want to take you out tonight!"

"Yeah, just give me a minute I have to get showered and changed."

Antonio said, yelling over the team. He hung up before I could say anything else. I asked Kylah if she wanted to tag along with Antonio and I, have a double date, but she said Chase had plans and that Angela was picking her up. After she left I sat there for 15 more minutes alone. As soon as I got up and started to call Antonio he swept me up off my feet and swung me around.

"Here I am, don't blow my phone up."

Antonio said carrying me through the crowd and outside to the car. We had small talk throughout the car ride, which, was prolonged because it was heavy traffic tonight. We finally got to the restaurant "Better eating." By the time we got to the door I noticed I didn't have my purse.

"Unlock the car." I said running back to the, "I forgot my purse."

I grabbed it off the front seat and ran back to the door to catch up with Antonio. He opened the door for me, the restaurant was busy, but not too bad so we were seated quickly.

The waiter came over and we both got water with lemon, by the time she came back we were ready to order. Antonio got spaghetti and meat balls, I joked about him being basic and he called me a lame for getting lasagna. Before our food came the waitress brought us side salads and bread sticks. I ended up regretting eating all the breadsticks before the food came because I only got a few bites in before I had to ask for a box. It only took seven minutes for Antonio to finish his food, he almost beat his record. It was a struggle for him to actually let me get the bill but he eventually caved. We left the restaurant a few minutes after some loud old people came and sat behind us. When we walked outside and Antonio went to unlock the car we noticed it wasn't locked in the first place.

"Somebody forgot to lock the door back when she got her purse. Cough, Cough." Antonio said jokingly as we got into the car. "Somebody's not getting a tip tonight."

We both laughed, I went to say something when I heard somebody laughing in the back seat. Antonio reached for the glove compartment and all of a sudden there was a hand over my mouth and a gun to my head.

"Drive."

Antonio started the car and pulled out of the parking lot. The guy in the back seat started laughing.

"Damn Antonio, we dating groupies now? I thought we just passed them."

Antonio slightly turned his head.

"Kevin? Are you fucking serious?"

"Yeah Skinner, Kevin. And yeah, I'm fucking serious. You turned soft of me huh boy? Back in the day, you would've killed me for stepping to you at the party, and I'm guessing your loss of monstrosity has everything to do with this fine piece right here. Actually, old you wouldn't have pulled out of the parking lot, you would've let me put shorty brain on the dash board and went on about your business."

Kevin pressed the gun deeper into my head. "I guess the pussy too good or something, right Skinner?"

Antonio didn't respond. I pushed back my tears because I knew if there was a time I needed to be strong, this was it.

"Take these next two rights then make a left into the empty lot."

As soon as we pulled in we saw two black trucks posted there with four guys standing in front of them. As soon as we parked and Antonio turned the car off, the men ran over and yanked him out of the car. Kevin pulled me out of the car himself and forced me to watch the men beat Antonio senselessly, still covering my mouth and holding the gun to my head. I couldn't stay strong once I saw them stomping on him. I bit Kevin's hand and he let go. I got the word

"Stop!" out before Kevin hit me with his gun and I fell to theground. He threw me next to Antonio, I heard him saying he

was sorry and that he didn't mean for me to get hurt. I cried uncontrollably. Kevin called off his boys and had one of them push the side of my face to the ground, making me watch Kevin stab Antonio. I screamed and tried to break free but I couldn't.

"Let this be a message for you, boy." Kevin said, spitting in Antonio's face. "Don't worry shorty, I hit him in every place I knew he wouldn't die."

He laughed and stepped over my body. His boys hit and kicked me a few times, making the injuries from Saturday even worse. I laid across from Antonio, seeing blood spill from his body. I couldn't move, I couldn't reach for him, I could barely say his name. I could feel myself drifting away, Antonio turned his head and I could see him trying to stretch his arm out to me right before everything went black.

The next thing I knew I woke up in a hospital room.

"Antonio?"

I called out as soon as I came to. I struggled to get the I.V out of my arm.

"Antonio! Baby!"

I said frantically. Two nurses ran in my room and pinned me down.

"Calm down! Calm down sweetie. Your ribs are broken and you have a major concussion, you cannot move right now."

"Antonio! Where is Antonio Rivet? Tell me, please!"

I said grabbing the nurses hand. They just looked at each other.

"Please." I said with tears rolling down my face. "Just tell me he's alive."

"Your friend is alive and stable, he just hasn't woken up yet. I'm sorry."

"No, no, no, no, no!"

I said, becoming frantic again. The nurses held me down and injected me with something, I was out like a light.

I woke up in what I thought was a few hours, but ended up being the morning. Kylah was by my side and Martin talking to Aaron in the hall way. I could barely open my eyes, I felt like I was being weighed down by a ton of bricks and my head was pounding,

"Kylah? Where's Antonio?"

"He just got out of surgery about an hour ago, he's awake and responsive."

Tears fell out of my eyes, every time I blinked I saw his blood filling the ground.

"What happened Kori?"

Kylah said as the nurse appeared. "You have a visitor." She said, opening the door wider. It was Curry, With flowers and bears.

"Kylah, give us the room please."

She hesitated, but got up and left the room. Curry put down the flowers and bears and took a seat next to my bed.

"I am so sorry, I promise you, I'm going to kill him myself Robin."

"I want... Let me help you."

"Nah, Robin. You need to hold down Skinner. I wanted to come see you first because even though Kevin put him in the hospital, he's not gone snitch. Who else was there helping him? What did they look like?"

"There was four other guys, all looked around 19-21. Three of them were black, one was white. Um... One of the black guys had glasses but he took them off. The white guy had tattoos on his hand. I don't know, it all happened so quickly. Kevin's boys did everything except stab Antonio, Kevin did that himself. Take me with you to see him. Please."

Curry grabbed the wheelchair from the other side of the room and carried me to it. To be the plug and a murderer, he did care about me. When I sat up in the wheel chair I really started to feel my broken ribs and concussion. I grabbed a blanket to put my face into so I could block out the light as we walked over to Intensive care. Curry got us through and we walked over to his room. I was so afraid to see him. Curry swung back the door and there he was... Laying there, staring at the wall.

"Baby?"

I said slowly rolling myself over to his side. He put his hand out and I grabbed it. He looked like he was in so much pain, he probably felt much worse.

"I love you." Antonio whispered. His entire face was swollen, he had gauzes and stitches all over his body. I couldn't stop looking at him, wishing I could take his pain and let him be healthy. Curry broke the silence.

"I'm going to kill him Skinner, Kevin and his boys." He said grabbing a bag of Antonio's clothes off the floor. His parents must be here somewhere.

"I know this won't help but I'm gone give you another 3grand. And I'm putting you off as my hit man. I threw a little extra in there for Robin too. When you get out of here I'm putting you as my eyes and ears. I'll pay you more then."

Antonio tried to speak, but I could tell the medicine they gave him made him drowsy. All he could do was nod his head before he drifted back to sleep. Curry left and I slowly got into the bed with Antonio. I couldn't sleep, so I laid there, listening to the monitor beep. Antonio's parents came in to drop off food, but they couldn't bear to see him in the hospital bed so they left. I had to go back to my room when they began to check his vitals, and I had to get mine checked as well. It was around noon and I was out right after they gave me medicine and food. Everybody seemed to have left, so I was alone, more alone than I already felt.

CHAPTER 15

I fell into a dream immediately. This one brought me joy. I was 5 months pregnant and Antonio was taking me to the doctor, we were having a girl. He'd just graduated and got his own apartment. Antonio said he wanted to make a stop before we went back to his place. We walked into a building and there was a huge baby shower waiting for me. My parents, my *real* parents were there smiling and holding gifts. It was amazing, Kylah and Chase were happy. We played games and nobody was stressed.

When I woke up reality set back in, my ribs ached and I had to breath slowly. My head was pounding, I was sensitive to light and sound. The beeping from the machines sounded like they were bull horns, and the light seemed like I was sitting next to the sun. Antonio was the only thought running through my head at that moment. Angela walked in moments later, she looked as if I was Kylah laying in the hospital bed. Her heels hitting the floor made me cringe, I deeply anticipated the moment she sat down. She sat on the edge of the chair next to me and ran her fingers through my hair.

"Are you okay?"

It seemed like the words came through my ears in slow motion. The light seemed to blind me and I fell into somewhat of a dream, a flash back of some sorts maybe. I was in a living room. It could've been the one at the house but I couldn't tell. Martin and Aaron were watching the news, Angela was talking about my parents, crying and it flashed over to photos of the accident. I started to get up from the couch and Martin rushed over to me, giving me a bear, the same bar that I saw in pretty much every photo and memory I had of my childhood. He ran his fingers through my hair and said

"Are you okay?"

I could hear Angela calling my name but I couldn't move or wake myself up from whatever was going on. I watched Martin walk back over to Aaron, they were talking but they must've gave me something to make me drowsy, everything seemed faint. I tried my best to hear what they were saying and disregard the news. All I could see was Aaron hand Martin two file folders.

"Burn them." Aaron said.

That's all I could make out. I just saw a bunch of moving, like they started arguing. Maybe he said he refused to burn the files, something that we didn't see. The last time Angela called out my name I responded.

"Hey, hey please. Be quiet, I have a horrible headache."

"Do you need anything?" Angela whispered. "Did you just think of something?"

I didn't know what to make of this, it wouldn't be long before I remembered anything. I didn't know how long I could keep up this act. I shook my head, she sat there for a few more minutes then got up to leave. It seemed like I could hear her heels click all the way to the parking garage. I'd finally gotten comfortable when Martin walked in.

"Hello Kori."

He said, walking swiftly to my side with that old bear.

"I see you're feeling better, dad."

I said with a sarcastic tone, he still looked busted and bruised and I enjoyed watching the pain pour from his face. He sat down in the chair next to my bed and just stared at me. I couldn't really match a description to the way he looked at me. I decided to break the silence with something I tried to ignore.

"So, who's Macey?"

He forced a surprised look, or maybe he honestly didn't remember that while he was trying to break every bone in my body he slipped up and called me by her name.

"Why do you ask darling?"

"I ask, because during your episode last Saturday you called me by that name."

"I think you already know the answer to that question darling. I'd be really careful if I were you. I don't know how, or why, but you're getting a little too damn close. I RAISED YOU!" He said slapping the arm of the chair. "Don't disrespect me. Look at the nice family we've become. You used to love dear old papa, now you look at me with such disgust and fear."

I couldn't believe what I was hearing.

"So y-you put…You put the lock on the door? You, kidnapped me?"

He began to laugh hysterically.

"Yes Cassie, and now I assume you want to know why?" He continued on. "I had a mother that loved to smack me around and a daddy that was too drunk to give a damn. I know, you may be wondering why I started drinking and why I began to smack people around. People tend to say you don't have to be a product of your environment but I never really had a chance. See I had a friend, once upon a time and I had Aaron. Aaron and I were subjected to the same abuse and well, my friend, unfortunately was in the same hell so, of course I grew up thinking that's all there was to life. But Phil, he wasn't strong enough, and a few days before our sixth birthday, because we shared a birthday, his mama decided she just didn't want to do it for another year. Aaron became so wrapped up in trying to stay alive he got an opportunity to leave to a boarding school and never looked back, I was alone. In the house, getting abused was lovely, beautiful, so you know I never had a chance. I took my first drink and I guess you can say my liquid courage and liquid anger jumped into me. I was grown and out the house, Aaron left and I had nobody. I met a sexy small town girl in the great state of Florida and boy did we fall in love. Whenever we would talk about babies it would make out heart rejoice, then she got pregnant. And then she lost the baby, *my baby*. Something in me snapped. Don't you think it was my turn? She was crying and crying like she was the one hurt. So I crushed up a bunch of pills, made sure they weren't invisible in her water, put on some music and we got into the bathtub. I felt the life rise from out of her and mine replenish. I'd already found you, honey. Turns out Aaron's shot at freedom didn't do him that well and he wanted to try again, so he cooked up some shit with a friend, pulled some strings and here we are baby. We're the Tuckers now, you're a Tucker now. Understand?"

I was completely stuck. I never thought he would ever admit it. His back story? Was it real? I couldn't gather words or push them out of my mouth. We just stared at each other. I felt my face relax and for some odd reason the tension lifted in the room. I wasn't afraid, I wasn't struggling to put matching pieces together, my mind wasn't in shambles. It was clear.

It's been cleared. The slate is clean. *I'm a Tucker now.* What can I really say about that? Testify? Stomp my feet? Declare war? As Cassie Powers I am an orphan. I'm dead, gone, forgotten, legally unaccounted for. What did I expect? I thought all these things and I still couldn't find the words.

"Understand?"

Martin repeated. I shook my head and took a breath to hopefully find the words, but a nurse came in saying Antonio was awake and wanted to see me. I jumped at the chance.

"Go home papa. I'll be fine here."

I saw the most sinful smile spread across his face. He kissed my forehead and tucked the bear in next to me. I watched as he walked away with his head high and a pep to his step. I slowly began to get out of my bed when Antonio was being brought through the door in a wheel chair with an IV pole following close after.

"How do I look?"

He said, trying to smile.

"Like the love of my life."

I slid into the chair next to my bed and put up the recliner so he could climb in next to me. I threw a blanket over us and we laid there, closer than ever. I broke the silence after a few minutes.

"What are you thinking about?"

I somewhat dreaded the answer.

"I'm just...I'm wondering why my parents didn't ask me why I was beaten an inch from my life. I wonder why I didn't just kill Kevin at the party or lock the car after you got your purse. I keep playing in my head how shitty I would feel if something worse happened to you, shittier than I already feel. I'm the animal!"

Antonio said hitting his chest.

"I protect you! I kill for you! But what happened? I'm lying next to you in your hospital bed. Kevin was right, I'm off my game. Baby don't take that the wrong way because you are my wife, my rider, the very reason my heart is beating right now. I want you to know, no I *need* you to know and understand that. We're going to be good, our baby is going to be good. Kevin will die for this, Curry said he'll take me off hit man too, for a while anyways, so I'm going to focus on us when we get out of here."

Antonio rubbed my stomach and I could feel him staring at me. I heard him and I wanted to respond, the words were sitting at the tip of my tongue, but I couldn't stop thinking about my dad. Even after all his indiscretions, so to speak, I truly did love him. I had no choice, regardless of how or why, he raised me. What do I tell Angela? He didn't insinuate that he knew she was helping me, but I don't need her help anymore. I want her to stop digging. She'll probably go ahead and pursue anyways. If I told my dad, he would probably destroy all evidence, but then again, she has some things in her possession. But what if I stole it? I still want the evidence in my back pocket, just in case... Right? I couldn't get out of my head. Antonio continued to talk but I couldn't hear.

"Hush baby."

I said putting my fingers over his lips.

"I hear you."

"So, you're just not going to respond to the answer to your question? Say I love you too? Did you really listen to anything I just said?"

I went to respond when Haley burst through the door.

"Hell no! Get out!"

Antonio said, still having to move slowly to get up. I grabbed his arm and pulled him back next to me. I couldn't risk having him rip stitches.

"You have 5 seconds to leave."

"Girl." Haley said, flipping her hair. "I just wanted to see if he was alive."

She walked over to the reclined chair and went to touch Antonio's face, he grabbed her hand and bent it back so far her wrist snapped and her body cringed.

"Keep your hands off me bitch. I don't know why you're here. I'm not your concern, you need to keep it pushing."

My eyes snapped open, I was not expecting that to come from his mouth. Apparently, neither did Haley.

"Antonio!"

She said with tears welling up in her eyes and grabbing her wrist.

"I am so sorry, please d-don't cry."

I just stared at them, staring at each other in shock

"Am I interrupting something?"

"No baby. She was just leaving."

Haley ran out of the room like someone just told her, her entire family died.

"What the hell was that about Antonio?"

"Baby, this is not the time we should be arguing, at all. It was nothing. She's nothing. You need to talk to me. Tell me what's on your mind."

I just ignored him, grabbed his hand and continued to lay there. We continued the routine every night until Antonio was released. We avoided conversation, but I could feel the intensity between us. It's been two and a half weeks. We had a home instructor bring our work to Antonio's house, I decided to stay with him. I was still a bit weary, about my father especially living with him. I still haven't decided what to do. Antonio's parents acted like nothing happened, they kept April at a distance and Antonio seemingly didn't notice. I guess my family isn't the only one wired different.

I kept thinking about two weeks before when Antonio and I decided to have a baby. While Antonio was sleeping I procrastinated taking the pregnancy test. I finally did, I paced around the bathroom waiting for the results. My heart raced as I picked it up. Positive. The test was positive. I had no idea what to say or how I actually felt. I made the decision quickly but I didn't quite weigh the options. I mean, Antonio loved me, he had plenty of money so that and taking care of the baby is fine in itself. But I am not in the person I said I was. Not that it was any of my fault but, I did find out and I did keep it a secret. I peeked out the door to see if Antonio was still sleeping, I decided to tell Kylah first.

"Hello?"

Kylah answered, sounded like she was eating chips or something.

"I'm pregnant."

"W-What?" She said coughing, "Are you serious?"

"Yes."

"Did you tell Antonio? What did he say? Wait. Martin! What is he going to say?"

I sat down on the small chair inside the bathroom.

"I don't know. I'll be over later."

She said ok and hung up the phone. I left the bathroom and walked over to Antonio's bed.

"Baby."

He tossed a few times before opening his eyes.

"Yes beautiful."

"I'm pregnant."

His eyes shot open and he shot up.

"Yes! Oh my God babe!"

He got on top of me and kissed me softly. He laid his hand over my stomach and held it there. He slowly inched down and pressed his lips against my stomach. After kissing it multiple times he whispered "Please stay. Be healthy. I want to love you."

It brought a tear to my eye. I hoped I didn't lose the baby. His mom lost three, Haley drunk herself into losing their kid... My father killed after the death of his child. I couldn't even think how my father, Aaron, Antonio's parents, how'd Curry respond, even... It's March 3rd, we've only known each other a few months, what would people think?

"Can you take me to see my dad? After we tell your parents?"

He picked me up and swung me around. I could tell the weight of me hurt him but he masked it well. We went downstairs and told his parents, they were shocked. They asked us if we were keeping it, Antonio seemed disgusted at the question and blew up. He threw me the keys and told me to get in the car and rushed back upstairs. When he came out he had three big bags.

"Baby, what are you doing?"

"I cannot believe they'd even insinuate I would let you get rid of the baby, or give it away? Never! I'm going to find us an apartment, but I'm getting a hotel until then. I brought a bunch of money and clothes for us.

"It's ok Antonio, they're just shocked, we are young babe."

His head snapped to the side, he grabbed my arm and pulled me close.

"I hope you're not saying you don't want this baby."

My mouth felt dry and my heart was pounding. I shook my head rapidly and put my hand over his.

"You're hurting me."

I said, looking him in the eyes. He quickly let me go, turned on the car and pulled off.

"We're going to see Curry first."

I didn't say anything. I could see this baby was a touchy subject for him. On the ride there I played how this day would go, over and over again, all different scenarios. We pulled up to Curry's house and there was an odd, strange feeling. When we walked in, everyone stopped moving, stopped talking. We walked straight back to Curry's room, as soon as we walked inside we saw Kevin. Antonio pushed me back into the wall and attacked him. I watched them fight. I watched Antonio turn into a monster. Curry sat there, watching him. Kevin fought back, but I could tell he was the type to shoot first and try not to swing. Antonio knocked him out, pulled out his gun and placed a silencer on it. He stood over him and watched him come to.

"What's up Kev."

He laughed and scooted up a few inches to lean against the wall. His mouth and nose gushed blood.

"You got me. Congratulations. I know you've waited for this moment. I see you got your groupie with you. Glad to see yawl made it out alive."

"What are you doing here?"

Antonio said, pushing the gun against his head.

"I came here to kill Curry, of course. I just wanted to talk first though. I know today is the day he gets his gun recycled and he's left alone without security detail but looks like I was wrong."

"It's time to put you down."

I walked toward Antonio slowly.

"You don't have to do this."

"JUST KILL ME ALREADY!" Kevin said, slapping the floor. "Stop being a bitch! DO WHAT I ALWAYS TAUGHT YOU TO DO! I built you from the ground up dammit! DO IT!"

His voice went from calm to yelling, and Curry just sat there. Watching it play out.

"Baby, turn around."

"NO!" Kevin screamed before I could respond. He pulled Antonio's hand closer to his head. "Put me down and let her watch!"

"Get up."

Antonio said, putting the gun into my hands. I pointed it at Kevin, not knowing what he was about to do.

"Oh, I get it." Kevin said laughing, with his hands up, letting Antonio strip him of his weapons. While he was checking him Kevin continued to talk.

"You know, I felt so empty when we met, when I took you under my wing I had already killed so many people." He said shaking his head and sighing. "I am so proud of you, I can't do it anymore, but you, whew. Don't let me down Toni."

I could see the doubt and hurt in Antonio's eyes. He walked closer to him.

"I could've come back to you or something. It didn't have to end like this."

Antonio walked around to the back of Kevin, and put his arm around his neck. I stepped back and watched the life leave from Kevin's eyes. A

126

smirk went across Antonio's face, and I watched as he slowly put his body onto the ground.

"I put you down."

I let go of the gun and stared at Antonio as he watched the gun hit the floor. He threw his hands over his face and dropped to his knees.

"I am so sorry."

CHAPTER 16

"I'll take care of clean up Skinner, you need to go."

Curry finally said, after his dead silence. Antonio drove over to my house in silence and I didn't break it. When we pulled up to the house I noticed Aaron's car in the driveway as well as my dad's. I walked slowly up to the door, Antonio following closely behind. When I went to grab the nob I had some kind of flashback again. I went back to being a little girl and was grabbing the handle. I snapped out of it quickly and walked in.

"Dad? Uncle Sandy?"

They both came rushing down the stairs but stopped in their tracks when they saw Antonio.

"What is this?"

My dad said, coming down the last few steps.

"I'm...Dad I'm pregnant."

"Are you fuc-."

"Stop!"

Aaron said, pulling back my father's hand.

"Pregnant?"

Aaron said, seemingly confused. Antonio grabbed my hand and slightly pulled me closer to him.

"It's Antonio's."

"No shit!"

"You don't have to be part of my child's life! You know how you *love* to take them."

Both their eyes shot open.

"Watch your mouth Kori." Aaron said.

"What is that supposed to mean baby?"

I didn't respond, I just stood there, waiting for the next comment.

"Ok. Ok. I- I want to be in this baby's life." Martin said, walking closer to me and putting his hand over my stomach.

"I'm sorry about the way things went between us." Antonio said. "I love your daughter and I'd do anything to protect her. I have the means and I will take care of her and the baby. I'm getting an apartment and I'll be graduating in a few months too."

My dad and uncle shook their heads.

"You plan on living with him Kori?"

"I don't know dad. After our encounters I don't think it'll be a bad idea."

"We need to talk about this. You need to stay here, alone."

I turned and gave Antonio the ok. He kissed me good bye and I told him I'd let him know when to pick me up. I followed my dad and uncle into the kitchen, staying on guard.

"She knows Aaron."

"How?"

"Because, I'm not stupid." I said, taking a seat. "How did you do it? How did you make me seem like I was his?"

Aaron scoffed,

"I'm not about to explain this to you. What are you planning to do? You going to go to the police?"

"You know I have flash backs of my childhood? I have vivid nightmares and hallucinations. I struggle to do simple things like stand in the shower, because I remember. I don't know who I am, who I could've been. Nothing. You were feeling sad because your girlfriend lost a baby, something she had no control over. So, instead of being there for her, you kill her. Then, you proceed to kill two loving parents and kidnap a child to fill a void? And then, this is where the story gets good. You get your equally messed up brother to cover your tracks, since he did such a good job there was no need to leave town, so you stay here! Not only do you stay here, but you date the friend of the mom whom you killed! Then, you abuse me, throughout my entire life, made me completely dependent upon you. You had to know keeping all those things in the house was a mistake. I'm lying to Antonio about who I am, I don't even know!"

"You are exactly who we raised you to be."

I couldn't believe I was actually having this conversation.

"You're not moving in with your boyfriend."

My father said, I rolled my eyes.

"This is not the time for you to be acting like father of the year, give it a rest."

"I love you! No matter what you think, I love you. I am so, so sorry for the things I've done, I have serious abandonment problems, anger issues, I know. Please, I want to be in your life. I don't want you to hate me. I don't know what you're thinking, but you could've went to the police a long time ago. So maybe you're looking out for yourself or you love us too, whatever it may be, you're here, and I need you."

I started to clap, it truly was a beautiful speech.

"Calm down uncle Sandy, I'm not going to call the cops. You can stop holding your breath now."

I pulled out my phone and told Antonio he could come back. When he texted me and said he was outside I got up slowly.

"I'll be back when I see fit. I'll go back to being the clueless Kori Tucker, pops, you can keep your hands to yourself and Uncle Sandy, be my savior, like always. K?"

They didn't respond, they just let me leave, I was glad it didn't go south. I walked out the door with my head held high, I was finally calling the shots. When I got into the car, Antonio couldn't keep his eyes off of me.

"Are you going to drive?"

I said sarcastically, breaking eye contact.

"You're not bothered by what you saw me do?"

"I'm not bothered by anything these days." I said putting my seatbelt on. "Can you go pick up Kylah?"

He shook his head, even though the doubt and confusion was written across his face. I called Kylah and told her we were on our way, of course she was at Chase's, so he'd be coming as well.

"Where do you want to go?"

"I don't know."

He pulled up to his house and they came outside almost immediately.

"So, you are going to tell me you were just joking, right?"

"No Kylah, I'm serious."

Chase started to laugh.

"Antonio, papa Toni."

I rolled my eyes, they were both being dramatic.

"Can somebody tell me where we're going?"

The car was silent.

"Can we go back to Curry's?"

I saw Chase squirm in the back seat.

"Who?"

Kylah said confused, I could tell she felt the intensity in the car.

"Kori, you should really chill out."

I kept my mouth shut while Antonio pulled off, I didn't know what was wrong with me. I lost all filters, my conscience was gone. I heard nothing. Nothing in the back of my mind, I didn't understand the silence.

"Um. Hello?" Kylah said, scooting to the edge of her seat to get closer to me and Antonio. "I am speaking English, right?"

Antonio responded quickly.

"I don't know who she's referring to."

I looked at Chase through the rear view mirror. He wore "Worried." Well. I laughed and continued to look out the window. Kylah's shoulders shrugged and she moved on to the next topic.

"What do you think it is? What did you want? Boy, girl? I'm excited, team god mom. Let me think of some names for you. Oh, the baby shower! Don't worry I'll plan. We have some months for that, we got to get you to a doctor, them prenatal vitamins and such. Girl, I wonder how you're going to look all big. I think th-."

Antonio cut her off.

"Please, shut up."

"Antonio! What is wrong with you!"

I said slapping his arm.

"It's ok, I talk when I get nervous."

"Why are you nervous?"

"I don't know, I'm excited too, I guess. Baby fever, yay!" She chuckled nervously "I'll stop talking."

Antonio pulled up at a red light and I turned around to look at Kylah's face. I started to laugh.

"Are you pregnant?"

Chase eyes jumped open.

"Hell no."

Kylah looked at Chase shocked, I couldn't stop laughing.

"Oh shit." Antonio said, shaking his head. "She didn't answer yet bro."

"I-I'm, I-I mean of course not."

Antonio pulled into the mall parking lot.

"You got money on you Chase?"

"Not that much, a band."

"Are you pregnant Kylah?"

I said, talking over Antonio and Chase.

"No! We're not ready for a baby anyways."

I looked at her confused.

"Come on Kylah, let's go shop."

Antonio handed me a couple hundreds and told me to wait for the rest. He and Chase stayed behind in the car for a while, for whatever reason.

"You have to go with me to get an abortion."

"Why? Why did you just lie?"

"Are you kidding Kori? Did you just see Chases' reaction when you asked me? How did you even know?"

I scoffed and walked into The Runway and picked up a shopping bag.

"I don't want the baby either."

"I take it, you two never talked about these consequences?"

Kyla rolled her eyes.

"I don't need a mother. I need a friend. I don't know, maybe this could just be a scare. I didn't actually take the test. I just haven't gotten my period."

"Well, after this store, you can take one. Then, tell Chase if it's positive. Now, help me pick some things out."

I started to feel it, that emptiness again. I tried to ignore it, but it seemed impossible. I didn't care about anything, I couldn't. We went into the drug store that was in the back of the mall, conveniently right next to a bathroom and got the test. I couldn't be bothered to get excited, or sad, whatever emotion I needed to show to be supportive to Kylah. I sat in the stall while she took the test and watched her pace while she waited.

"It's negative!"

She said jumping up and down. I forced a smile.

"Yay, no abortion!"

She rolled her eyes and threw away the test, that was an irrelevant and misguided venture. We ran into Antonio and Chase browsing in the sneaker store. Kylah and I sat there while they picked out shoes.

"So, what we doing for our birthday?" She said excitedly. "It's our big 18!"

"They're two days apart. It's not our birthday."

Kylah rolled her eyes.

"It basically is Kori. What's your problem today?"

"I really don't know. I'm just stressed. We can do anything for our birthday, you can choose."

I put my face into my hands and unknowingly let myself slip into a day dream. I was on the couch at home, crying, asking for my mom. Martin brought me food and candy every hour on the hour. It seemed like I would never stop crying, until I did. Why did I? Maybe I couldn't remember why I was crying after a while, why I was scared. If my actual reality was reality at all. I longed for people that didn't exist. They did, they were very much alive, and I'm not sure how I feel about it. I'm Kori Tucker, I'm all I know how to be. I guess. I quickly jerked myself out of my thoughts when I felt Antonio's touch.

"You ok baby?"

He said, caressing my leg. I shook my head and got up, pushing my feelings to the side.

"Angela just called. I got to be home soon."

We spent about an hour more in the mall, shopping and getting food before taking Kylah home, and taking Chase to Curry's.

"What were you thinking earlier? You were about to tell Kylah about Curry? You can be upset all you want but our problems don't have anything to do with her."

I just sat there in silence, thinking about the lack of emotion there actually was. When we got to Antonio's house, no one was home, so I knew this would continue on. We made it all the way into his room without a word, but as soon as the door shut he went off like clock-work.

"So, you're not going to answer me?"

"There's nothing to say Antonio, I forgot she didn't know, it was my mistake."

"What is your problem? You've been acting strange all day, is it the pregnancy? Is it me? Something I did, or your dad and uncle did?"

I shook my head. I knew he'd never understand. The way he grabbed me earlier, made me think twice about bringing up my doubts about the baby. I couldn't tell him my dilemma about my dad and uncle. He would be confused if I told him I felt empty. So I got into bed and laid down, disregarding what he was saying. He climbed in next to me and held me, quietly. As soon as he tightened his hold I knew I couldn't keep my tears pushed back. The first tear fell and hit Antonio's arm, then a few more after. When he noticed he turned my face to make me look at him and wiped my tears.

"Why are you crying?"

"Just a lot on my mind, I don't really want to talk about it."

Antonio shook his head and threw the cover over me.

"I can take your mind off of it?"

He laid behind me and pressed my body up to his, pulling down my pants in the same swift motion. He kissed down my back and left hickeys in between my thighs, came back up and kissed my neck.

"I can take your mind off of it?"

He repeated, I slightly nodded yes and he slid inside, making my eyes roll into the back of my head. He'd never been so gentle and soft but controlled at the same time. He pinned my arms behind my back but continued to stroke deeply and slowly. He threw my legs open every time they would clench, but ate me like it's be his last meal. We went for hours. After, we laid there, talking about the baby, living together, what we'd do after I graduated. It was pushing 7 by the time anybody came into the house. We'd ordered food and gotten settled by then. Antonio got a text from Curry saying he had a hit for him.

"So much for putting you off for a while."

I said, watching him put his things on.

"Are you coming?"

"Are you going to let me do this one?"

I longed to know how it felt. Antonio hasn't been too happy with my curiosity, but I wanted to do it.

"You don't know what you're asking."

I rolled my eyes.

"Yes I do."

Antonio put on a shirt and got on top of me.

"You do?"

He said slowly running his hand down my face. I shook my head. I closed my eyes when he leaned down for a kiss, instead, I felt his hands wrap around my neck. He began choking me, I could see his face but it was blurry. I scratched and slapped his arm trying to release myself and I felt the last breath dissipate from my lungs. When my eyes began to close he let go, and I shot up coughing, trying to catch my breath.

"You don't know what you're asking. You can't do that to someone.

The way you just felt your life slowly leave your body? Nah, you're not built for it."

"You just tried to kill me."

"No I didn't. There is no try. I wanted to show you what it felt like on the other side."

He turned his back to me and sat down at his desk. I grabbed his pocket knife from his drawer. I slowly walked over to him and hugged him from behind.

"You're right."

I said, kissing the back if his neck. He started to breathe heavily and threw his head back to see me. I pressed the knife to his neck and kissed him softly. He didn't move, He just stared into my eyes. I slowly and carefully dragged the knife across his neck in one long stroke.

"I'm built for that. Baby."

He took the knife from my hand and threw it across the room, grabbing me and slamming my face into the wall. He wrapped a chunk of my hair into his hand and pulled it hard.

"You could've killed *me*."

He was very turned on by that. He couldn't control himself. I felt his demeanor change, he shifted into his monster alter ego. He lifted me like I was a feather, but before he could begin to start round 6 Curry called him back to back. Antonio put me down and punched the wall.

"Fuck!" He said, striking the wall a few more times and turning around to look me up and down. "Get dressed."

I smiled and got my clothes on. I watched Antonio get his guns together, he made me wear a purse so I could hold his money and my gun, so he wouldn't have to carry a duffel bag.

CHAPTER 17

We got into the car and went to Curry's quickly. When we walked in everything was back to normal.

"Robin! Good to see you, how you holding up?"

I just smiled and nodded.

"What's the hit Curry?"

"Well Skinner, this one is a girl, a white girl. I don't need you to kill her. I need you to fuck her for some information on the where a bouts of her brother. The information is either in her phone or somewhere in her room. Get that."

"Yo, Curry, my girl is standing right here! What the hell is wrong with you?"

"Well, see that's the issue. Baby Snow, she's gay."

My eyes jumped open.

"No, hell no, not happening."

Antonio said, shaking his head.

"I mean, I'll do it. It's just a girl, can't be that bad, plus, I'm open minded."

Antonio looked shocked.

"Really bae? Am I hearing you correctly?"

Curry laughed obnoxiously.

"Damn, where was a girl like you at for me?"

Curry got the file from the desk and slid it to the edge with three stacks of money on top.

"That's for you Robin. All of it, and I heard Snow a bit of a freak, might want to bring a friend. She's always at Bongos, the club downtown. Say yes, make it easy."

I looked at Antonio, looking back at me.

"No." Antonio said sternly.

"No?" Curry said.

"No, I don't want her involved."

"Get with it boy. This is what I'm asking you to do. Fuck your feelings about her cheating or whatever petty shit is in your head. This is the job boy. Get it done."

"It's not about that."

"Then what is it about?"

"She's not doing it!"

Antonio yelled, Curry's boys went to grip their guns when Curry told them to chill. Antonio grabbed my hand and walked out. We didn't talk about it on our way back to the house, he just acted like it didn't happen. I tried to understand where he was coming from. Maybe he did consider it cheating, or maybe he was weary because he couldn't be there to participate. Maybe it was because I was pregnant, but I was only 3 weeks, or because he knew I'd ask Kylah. I don't know. I couldn't wrap my head around it. I wanted to help though, I wanted to explore. I tried to discuss it with myself, but my conscience was gone, all my guidance, the devil and angel on my shoulder was gone. When Antonio left to go get us more food I called Kylah.

"Hello?"

She said, answering on the first ring.

"Are you alone?"

"Yeah, why?"

"You ever been with a girl?"

The phone was silent for a few moments.

"Um. No? Why? Wh-what's going on?"

"Do you want to be?"

"What?" She said in a confused but amused tone. "Are you coming on to me?"

"I am."

The phone went silent for a few more moments, and then Kylah responded.

"Since when do you want to be with me like that? Since when do you want to be with any girl like that?"

"Yes or no?"

"Yes."

I looked at the phone to make sure I was talking to Kylah.

"Y-yes?"

"When?"

"Uh, um well, this girl everyone calls Snow invited me to a little party. Just us though."

"Ok, call me with details."

"Kylah?" I said after a long pause. "Have you thought about being with me before?"

She laughed, "Yeah, plenty of times."

She hung up before I could respond. I dropped the phone and stared at it in awe. A little smile came across my face.

"Well, I'm flattered."

I whispered to myself. I laid there and fantasized until I had to snap myself back to reality when Antonio came back in with food.

"What are you thinking about?"

Antonio said, putting everything down. I just smiled and got the chicken sandwich and fries out the bag. We ate and watched movies as usual. This was our last weekend before we stopped home instruction. Antonio fell asleep around 11 and I soon followed suit. When we had to wake up for school we both dragged like zombies. We showered together, got dressed together and went to get breakfast. We were right on time for the late bell. When we walked in everybody acted like they'd seen a ghost and Antonio and I were more popular than before. When I saw Kylah she nodded her head, telling me to come to the bathroom with her. Antonio kissed me on the cheek and disappeared into the crowd of boys and their groupies.

I walked slowly to meet Kylah. When I opened the door and looked at her, I saw lust fill her eyes.

"So, you were serious?"

She said checking the stalls to see if anyone was in them.

"Yeah, dead serious."

"So who is this Snow you refer to?"

"Just some girl that made me wonder is all."

Kylah walked closer to me. I wondered how long she had these feelings for me. She didn't say anything, she just stared at me, at my lips really. After a few seconds of intense staring, she kissed me. I closed my eyes and kissed her back. She got so close I could feel her heart beating. The kiss lasted a while until Kylah broke away.

"Was it everything you imagined?"

I said, watching her touch her lips, like she was surprised at what we just did.

"It was better. Was it good for you?"

I smiled and kissed her again. This time it went beyond a kiss. She bit my lip and slipped her tongue into my mouth. I opened my eyes but immediately closed them back. I didn't expect to be so comfortable with this. I though it's be weird since she was my best friend but it wasn't. I grabbed her butt and she pulled back in shock again. I could feel my body reacting to her tenderness. Kylah smiled and chuckled.

"Who are you?"

I gave her another peck and returned the laugh.

"I don't know."

We heard some girls gather around the door so we separated ourselves. Kylah stared at me all the way until she got out of the bathroom but I stayed behind. I didn't quite know what to think of what just happened. It was good, it felt right…Well not right but, not wrong. I closed my eyes and I immediately saw my child self, inside of my room. I could hear Martin talking to Aaron saying

"We're going to call her Kori."

After he said that it kept echoing over in my head. When I opened my eyes I began to think about what Kylah said. I knew her asking me who I was had no relation to what I was actually thinking but when I said I didn't know, I actually didn't. I wanted to feel something inside again and I wanted to reinvent myself. Not going by the name that was taken from me or the name that was given to me. I walked on egg shells and did what I was told my whole life. I wanted to act on impulse, I think. I wanted to be myself, I think, whatever that meant.

I released myself from my thoughts and went to class. I was glad my grades stayed up during home instruction so I could just carry on with the rest of the class. My birthday is on Friday so I pushed through the week. Kylah and I didn't discuss when we'd be going to see Snow or our kiss after that day, but she, Antonio and Chase skipped school with me to celebrate my birthday right. We went out to eat, went to play paint ball and went to the beach together. Antonio bought be giant balloons with hearts and the mos gigantic 18 you could imagine. With money, of course, a handwritten card, new lingerie and everything. It was a great day, I went home that night and my dad and uncle were waiting up for me. When I walked in the both held up a cake with 18 candles. We put our problems to the side that night, ate cake and watched a few movies together. I really did love them, even though I wasn't supposed to meet them, or be their daughter and niece. I didn't know though, maybe this was always part of my life's plan. Whether it was or wasn't I was still there, with them and my parents were still dead.

When I woke up in the morning the house was empty. Antonio hadn't text me so I was glad I didn't have to lie to him. I got in the shower and got dressed, about an hour later I took a bus over to Curry's alone. When I walked in he was surprised to see me. I tried to feel bad about what I was about to do, I was even trying to talk to some inner self I had to make her talk me out of it. There was still silence and an absence of emotion.

"Robin, fancy seeing you here without Batman by your side."

"I came to get the file and the money. I have a friend and she's down to pay a visit to your snow bunny."

A sinister smile rose on his face.

"I do recall Skinner saying no deal. Does he know you're here right now?"

I smacked my teeth and rolled my eyes, and ignored his comment. He took the hint, he got everything out of his desk and handed it to me.

"I'm going to have a car pick you up, when you're ready, just dial this number."

"I trust this will stay between us."

Curry laughed and shook his head. "I have no idea what you're referring to."

I nodded my head and put the money and file into my bag and returned home. I text Kylah and told her to come over. She was there in less than an hour. She had her hair in tight curls and had on red lipstick and tight clothing. I never noticed how attractive she actually was. Her blue eyes were brought out with her make-up and blended perfectly with her freckles.

"Damn."

I said moving out the way so she could come inside. She followed me upstairs and watched me get dressed. I put on lace underwear and a tight latex body suit. I pinned up my hair and curled the ends. I took off

Antonio's chain and the ring he gave me and put on a choker necklace and watch. I sprayed myself down with perfume and looked in the mirror. I was unrecognizable to myself. I shrugged the feelings off and called the number Curry gave me. When I got the ok to go outside I turned off my phone and grabbed Kylah's hand. The ride over there was silent, but I couldn't keep my eyes off Kylah.

The club was already packed for it to be 1 in the afternoon. I looked at the picture of Snow and scanned the room. When I saw her my heart began to race. She was extremely beautiful, and an older woman. Only about 22 or 23 but, established and grown. Kylah stayed pressed to me the entire time we walked across the room. We ignored all the men trying to get at us and buy us drinks. As soon as we got in Snows line of sight she fixed her eyes on us. We walked up to her table and took a seat.

"I see you watching me."

I said seductively, watching Kylah shift into character.

"We want to play."

Kylah said, whispering in her ear.

"They call me Snow." She said, grabbing her purse. "Let's play."

I smiled and grabbed her hand to lead her to the car. When we got in she told the driver to go to her house on Hanson avenue. She was clearly wealthy. She was paying special attention to Kylah, I think she was more attracted to her.

"So, you ladies going to introduce yourselves?"

"They call me Shotty."

I said, looking over to Kylah, hoping she got the hint.

"They call me Missy."

"Well, Shotty and Missy." Snow said licking her lips. "Welcome to my play pin."

We pulled up to her house and my jaw dropped. It was an actual mansion. We walked inside and followed Snow up to one of the many master bedrooms they had. Snow immediately dropped the fur coat she had on. She had black and red lingerie underneath, it went perfectly with her designer heels.

"Strip ladies."

I laid on the bed and Kylah took my clothes off.

"I need help unzipping mine."

Kylah said turning around. I went to do it when Snow took over, saying she had it covered. She unzipped her skin-tight, silk dress all the way to the end and pulled down each side slowly. She kissed Kylah's back and pushed her onto the bed next to me. I stared at Kylah while Snow took her panties off. Kylah pulled my hand down so I could feel how wet she was. I pushed my fingers inside and watched as Kylah's back arched. Snow went on the other side of me and kissed my neck, slowly making her way to my lips. Snow guided my hand from Kylah and held it as she sat on my face. She was already dripping. I started to eat her immediately, I did better than I thought I would. I felt Kylah's warm tongue going in circles around my nipples, I quivered as she worked her way down. I could tell she'd waited a long time for that. It was amazing. We went a few hours switching positions, trying a lot of them too, way more than I thought was possible considering there were only girls. Snow was the first to tap out, she sat across the room and continued to watch Kylah and I.

We finished together. After, Kylah got up and joined Snow in the chair. Snow had such a crush on Kylah. They decided they wanted to take a shower together. I told them to start without me, that I could hardly feel my legs, but I really just wanted to snoop around. I got her phone out of her fur coat but there was nothing. I looked around in her dressers and found a planner. She had a day marked off every Wednesday that said "Brother" with an address. I quickly took an empty page from the back, wrote everything down and put it back. After I was done, I followed the path of roses Snow laid out and went to finish playing. We stayed there until 5 something in the afternoon. Snow gave Kylah her number and told us both to come back some other time. I called the driver back and Kylah and I left. When we got into the car I was relieved and excited.

"That was amazing."

Kylah said, wrapping her hair up.

"Yeah, it was."

The ride to Kylah's was silent. When she got out, she kissed me goodbye. I hoped she didn't think this would be a recurring event between us, but I kind of figured she did and I wasn't sure if I was actually bothered. I got in the front seat with the diver, whom was Curry's security detail. We pulled up to the house and I went straight back.

"Look who it is."

"I got it."

"Mm. Quick and efficient. Let me find out I should get you permanently. Let me see."

I showed him the address and told him that they meet every Wednesday, after he wrote it down I turned around to leave.

"Don't go yet Robin, come chill with me and some of my crew."

I was nervous, but I didn't have anywhere to be. Curry got up and I followed him into another part of the house. He had a screen room where there was a lot of men and woman smoking, talking, and doing deals. I was definitely fitting in. After an hour. I remembered I turned my phone off. When I turned it on again it started ringing off the hook with notifications. Antonio called me 32 times, Kylah called me 5 times and my dad called me 12. I quickly asked Curry's driver to take me home. Luckily, my dad was just concerned with my safety. I showered and called Antonio back. He was angry that I didn't answer or call him all day but he jumped at the chance to come and get me. When I saw him he couldn't take the smile off his face.

"I've been thinking about you all day."

He said, continuing to smile. I forced myself to smile back.

"I'm really tired baby. You mind if we just go straight to your house?"

Antonio shook his head and pulled off quickly, he kept that speed all the way to his house. He carried me up the stairs and put me into bed.

"You're so good to me." I said, grabbing his hand. "You're going to get into bed with me, right?"

"Of course, and you deserve to be treated like the queen you are."

He stripped down into shorts and got into bed. He put his hand on my stomach and a huge smile came across his face.

"I'm going to be a dad."

I smiled and actually began to come to terms with the pregnancy. Just the fact that I'm actually going to be a mother. He laid there with me, telling me about his day, and how he ran into some people from his childhood. It was nice to just listen for once, and I was glad I didn't have my conscience to weigh on me. Antonio and I stayed up to at least 3 in the morning. When we finally went to sleep we didn't wake up until 12 in the afternoon. When Antonio got up to shower I decided to call Kylah back but she didn't answer, she was probably with Chase or getting ready for her birthday party. Angela decided to throw her one last minute. Good thing Kylah is popular and word got around fast or it wouldn't have been the best turn out, then again, who would miss a 18 and older birthday blow out? I picked out my clothes and paced around until Antonio got out the shower. After he got dressed he told me lunch would be ready by the time I got out of the shower and clothed.

I was excited for Kylah's party. I knew she'd wanted one. We ate and then drove over to Kylah's. When we walked in Chase was there blowing up balloons, Antonio went over to help him. Kylah was in the kitchen setting up, blasting music, so I walked in and surprised her.

"Happy birthday best friend."

I said, handing her 1,800 just to add some zeros on her age, and a singing card.

"Damn, I must be one hell of a best friend." She said winking at me. "We're both legal!!!!! I'm ready to party!"

Kylah said laughing and jumping up and down. I washed my hands and helped her set up her chocolate bar and bake. I was glad that everything was still normal between us. After a few hours of setting up, decorating and getting food, the party was finally going to start. Kylah went upstairs to put on her party clothes while Antonio, Chase and I greeted people at the door. When Kylah came back downstairs, the party really started. It seemed like everyone was there. I kept catching her stare at me through the corner of my eye, but I couldn't look her in her face. Every time I did I pictured her in between my legs. I kept thinking about how good she looked without clothes and every foul thought possible flowed through my mind.

CHAPTER 18

Kylah got tons of gifts and everybody but me was drunk. The party didn't end until 4 and everyone there pretended we didn't have school in the morning. It was going to be a lot of absences and a very boring school day for people who actually went. Antonio, Chase and I all stayed at Kylah's because Angela never came home and Antonio was drunk. I was awake with morning sickness and everyone else was simply hung over. Around 2pm we helped Kylah clean up the mess then headed back over to Antonio's house. When we got back, we showered and I made sure Antonio wore off his drunk. About an hour went by when Curry called him over. We went almost immediately. I was a bit nervous walking in but I knew Curry wouldn't blow my spot up.

"Well isn't this my favorite couple. Don't you two ever get a break from each other?" Curry winked and continued. "Well, doesn't matter. Now, let's get down to business. I got the information for your hit, now I need you to get this done in two weeks max. He's a threat to my business so you need to be swift and precise."

"How you get this information?"

Curry's security that was the driver laughed and coughed sarcastically. Antonio was about to say something when Curry cut him off,

"You're questioning me boy? After that shit you pulled last time you were here, disobeying my orders you best be on your best behavior. Isn't that right?"

I could feel Curry's security staring at me since he drove me around yesterday. There was a certain tenseness between Curry and I that I tried to ignore. I was just ready to leave.

"Whatever man."

Antonio said, collecting his money.

"What's up Robin." Curry said winking. "Nothing to say today?"

I shook my head and kept eye contact until Antonio finished copying the information and we left.

"He just talked to me Friday, how the hell did he get this information? He can be such an ass hole sometimes."

Antonio said getting into the car. I didn't respond, I just got in and put my seat belt on.

"I don't know what Curry's man was laughing at, nothing I said was a joke."

I began to scoot down in my seat with every word he said. He pulled off and continued to talk.

"You ever gone tell me why you didn't get any of my 32 calls Saturday? When I went to Kylah's yesterday Chase said she was missing too. I guess yawl both disappeared on the same day."

Antonio laughed and continued to drive. We got to his house and went up to his room. I was sitting on the bed when I saw Antonio scratching his head.

"What are you doing?"

"You know what I just thought about? Why the fuck you and Kylah disappeared the day after I told Curry you weren't going to get with that bitch Snow bunny."

My eyes shot open.

"Coincidence?"

"Do I look stupid to you Kori? Did you take Kylah to go fuck Snow?" I stood up and Antonio got in my face. "ANSWER ME!"

"I am so sorry."

I watched Antonio's shoulders drop.

"No. No, no. You didn't. Please, Kori, you didn't do this to me!"

"I did, I did baby I'm so sorry." I forced tears down my face. "I-I was just trying to help."

I went to grab his hand but he snatched away from me.

"Don't! Don't fucking touch me."

His voice sent chills down my spine. I saw tears well up in his eyes, I knew he was hurt, but I could not attach myself emotionally or naturally.

"What did I ever do but love you! Everything I ever did was for you! Why did you do this? Why did you let me love you?"

He said as he put everything of mine inside duffel bags.

"Baby, please let's just talk about this. We've been doing so good together. Please, this can't be what breaks us apart. Think about the baby."

"We have been doing good, but this is what will break us apart. Not only did you cheat on me, but you brought Kylah into something I'm 100% sure she didn't know was bigger than a good time. You went to Curry's alone, you got 3 racks alone, you're the reason I'm about to kill this man. The worst part is, you don't even know you've done something wrong. I am thinking about the baby, but you weren't! You had sex with someone other than me PREGNANT! You put you and my baby at risk. Don't worry, I'm still going to take care of it, but you and me? We're done."

I tried to reason with him, but he wouldn't hear it. As soon as the first tear escaped from his eye he went crazy. He punched three holes in the wall and screamed with each blow. I just stood there, watching. Antonio dropped to his knees.

"Do you even care! Damn, who are you! Who the fuck is you! I don't even recognize you."

I got onto the floor with him.

"Please, baby. I am so sorry, everything been hard for me. Please, I can't lose you."

Antonio looked at me like I had just twisted the knife.

"Things have been hard for you? HOW! What did I do? I know, being in the hospital wasn't ideal but I have been there for you and I went through that too, but you don't see me doing things behind your back. I loved you, I fucked you on the regular, I gave you money, I took you shopping, I talked, I listened. When you said jump I said how high. So what is it! Please, tell me. Right now you're another Haley except I actually gave a damn about you. Give me an excuse right now that could soften this hurt and make me feel like I wasn't the dumbest nigga on earth for giving you a seat in the cafeteria that day."

I didn't respond, I just sat there, staring at him. He got up abruptly and punched the wall again.

"Answer me! Answer me right now! I deserve it!"

He yelled over and over again. I burst into tears. I cracked.

"While I was in the hospital...Martin told me I wasn't who I thought I was... That he and my uncle killed my parents and took me for themselves.

After that, I got confused. I didn't know if I wanted to be angry or if I was ok. I don't know who I am. My reality was snatched from under me and I cracked. I am so sorry."

I watched Antonio's entire demeanor change. There was a quick swarm of calmness that over powered him.

"I don't believe you."

His words felt like a thousand daggers hit me in the heart at once. He reached over and snatched his chain from my neck.

"Get out."

I watched him turn and walk away from me. This was real, we were seriously broken up. I could literally feel the emotions return to my body. Tears streamed down my face and I couldn't move. I was stuck. I heard Antonio slam his car door and pull off. I sat there and paced around his room, trying to decide whether or not I should wait for him to return. I decided against it, the way he looked at me and the size of the holes in the wall, it was my best bet to leave.

On my walk home I played the conversation over and over inside my head. The way he dropped to his knees and when his voice cracked made me feel the worst. It took me almost a half hour to get home. When I walked inside I went straight to my room and locked the door. I'd run out of tears by then. I laid there, staring up at the wall. I shut my eyes tight, in hopes that when I opened them I would be hysterical and broken out in sweats. I prayed to anybody that would listen that this was a dream, and that Antonio would come back to me. That wasn't the case. The room was completely dark now that I'd closed the curtains to block the light from outside. I let myself fall asleep.

The dream began with Kylah and I at Snow's house. It repeated every action up until Kylah and Snow went to take a shower. After I wrote down her brother's address, I fell through the floor. I ended up in what seemed to be an interrogation room, except I could see out but no one could see me. I watched Antonio talk to Curry, then I watched as he went over to the brother's house. I watched him beat him for hours to get information on who else was in the plan against Curry. After Antonio got it, he beat him to death with his bare hands. He was dancing around and having fun with it. I heard a voice echoing in the background telling me that I did it. I was the reason somebody's son and brother was being brutally murdered.

I began screaming and I laid my head down, only to feel myself shift into a different position. When I lifted my head I was in the house with My father and Macey, watching him mix the drugs into her drink. He looked to the side, this time I was able to be seen.

"Soon you'll be just like me."

He said, walking to the bathroom. I began crying again. I ran to the bathroom to try to stop him but I didn't work.

"I'm nothing like you!"

I said, dropping to my knees. I heard another voice echoing in the back of my head.

"You're nothing like him? Then who are you? Not my little girl Cassie. You're the monster they raised you to be."

I started banging my head into the wall, over and over until I couldn't see anymore. There were different voices laughing viciously in my head. I tried to scream but I was muffled. I forced myself awake and couldn't move because my head hurt so bad. I just continued to lay there in the dark, alone. I replayed the moment I started to be suspicious of my father, the moment I got my first piece of the puzzle. I began recalling the first sign I had of PTSD and when Antonio and I got serious. Every moment before this has been leading up to the position I was in. I finally produced more tears and cried myself back to sleep.

I didn't have any more dreams but I woke up every hour on the hour until my alarm went off in the morning. I turned my alarm off and sunk deeper into the bed, throwing the sheets over my entire body, I couldn't force myselfto get up for school and I couldn't face anyone. I ignored my father and uncle's knocks on the door in attempts to get me in school and continued to lay there. I didn't move at all for hours. I listened to cars go by and heard conversations of the people passing by. There was a life outside my four walls that I complexly detached myself from and could no longer deal with. I ignored calls and texts from everyone and continued to lay there until I heard Antonio's ringtone. I jumped up and answered immediately.

"Hello?" There were several moments of silence on the other end. "I can hear you breathing Antonio."

He cleared his throat.

"You weren't in school. I had to make sure you didn't die last night. I see you're very much alive, so."

I went to respond but he hung up too quickly. I called right back but it went to voicemail after 2 rings. I returned back to the same spot and continued to drench the bed with my tears. An hour after school let out

Kylah knocked on my bedroom door, begging me to let her in. I did, then got right back into the same spot.

"You look horrible. What happened?"

"Antonio and I broke up."

She ran her fingers through my hair.

"Why? What…" She paused then continued. "Oh."

I started crying and she leaned over and began kissing me. I brushed her off, but she soon started again. When she kissed me before I felt chills but I felt nothing but a deep and sudden sense of shame.

"Kylah, you need to stop. I can't do this with you."

She rubbed my face and a few moments later began to move downwards slowly, but I quickly grabbed her wrist.

"I said no Kylah."

She seemed shocked and I immediately saw the hurt in her eyes.

"Why not? What's changed since our kiss in the bathroom and Snow's house? I thought… I thought this is what you wanted. I thought you loved me."

I felt my heart fall into my stomach.

"I do love you. As my best friend. I think you're beautiful and amazing but… I love Antonio. We did what we did because I was being selfish, trying to fill a void in myself and twisting around logic so it'd make sense in my head. I ended up hurting him and you. I'm sorry. I hope you can forgive me."

She jumped off the bed and stared at me with tears falling from her eyes.

"So that's it then? I was just an experiment to you? You brought me into your shit so you could feel better? You laid down with me and looked at me like you'd been feeling the same way about me." Kylah laughed. "That's great."

"Kylah, I'm being serious. I know I shouldn't of lead you on, I was wrong. At least I told you instead of continuing a relationship I don't want just to spare your feelings."

"AND YOU'RE GOING TO KEEP SAYING IT! I get it Kori. You don't want me. I could've given you a better love than Antonio, but I guess you wanted to make a fool out of me instead. I *never* want to see or hear from you again."

She turned to walk away when I grabbed her arm.

"Please, you're all I have left."

She snatched away and wiped her tears. There was nothing but anger left.

"Fuck you Kori."

I felt the last bit of life inside my body fall to pieces as I watched Kylah storm out. My face was raw from the tears and every bone in my body ached. I locked my door again and fell face first into my pillow. I cried, tossed and turned. I sat there thinking of how I could fix this. I couldn't wrap my head around the fact that I had no one. I laid on my back and stared into the darkness. My stomach felt like it was popping, I laid my hand on it and imagined A happy family. Every time I shut my eyes and saw Antonio's face I cried harder. I whispered "sorry" until I fell back asleep. Of course, I had a nightmare.

I was in a cold and damp basement. I couldn't see for a while until a bright like turned on. My baby was on a screen above me, screaming

"Why'd you have to do it mommy? Why? Everybody hates you now."

Over and over again. I cried hysterically. I searched around the room for the source of the video. I crawled around and looked for cords, a door, anything. I'd been looking around for several minutes until someone grabbed me out of nowhere. I shut my eyes tight until I felt myself being thrown on to a wooden chair. The light was even brighter now, I could barely open my eyes to look around. I heard Antonio's voice in the distance.

"You hurt me. You hurt me so bad Kori."

I cried out to him, but I went unanswered. I heard heels hitting the floor and the sound seemed much closer now.

"It's ok, she hurt me too. Now we both can take care of it."

"Kylah?"

I said, confused and trying to see where they were. I heard them both laughing. After a few seconds the sound came to a dead stop. I screamed but I heard nothing back. I felt rope begin to dig into my skin, they got so tight I lost circulation. I heard a loud whisper, but the words being uttered were unclear. I heard a gun cock back and the whispers began to grow louder and harsher. I could no longer feel my arms and I noticed the light was dimming.

"Hello! Please! I'm sorry. I'm so sorry."

I struggled to set myself free. I screamed louder and louder every time it would get darker. The light was nearly off when I saw Antonio and Kylah holding hands. They both had guns pointed at me. Antonio shot first and it went passed my ear, Kylah followed suit. I watched as the both looked at each other and laughed. The monitor with my baby turned on again. This time, it was standing in front of the camera, holding it.

"They missed on purpose mommy. Bye, now."

I went to scream when I felt a bullet hit my chest. Antonio and Kylah walked over to me and kissed both sides of my cheek. Antonio grabbed my hand as Kylah pushed the barrel deep into the middle of my head. I shut my eyes to brace myself for the shot. I saw Martin, he yelled

"Open your eyes Cassie, Open your eyes Kori."

As soon as I opened my eyes, my chair began to move rapidly towards him. When I got close enough to see his face, he reached his arms out to grab me. I was inches away when I heard Kylah pull the trigger and I fell into the light.

My eyes shot open and I heard my notifications going off. I threw my phone against the wall and sat up in bed. I was drenched in sweat, my hair was a mess, my head was pounding and my face felt skinless. I slightly opened the curtain to make sure I was home alone.

I slowly unlocked my door and walked down a few rooms into the bathroom. I fell to the floor next to the tub and filled it. I stripped out of my clothes and slipped in. I sunk down into the bath and closed my eyes. I played the dream over in my head, then, my thoughts shifted to my parents. I pictured their faces and imagined that I had memories of them, actual memories of them, waking me up in the morning, reading me stories. I thought about how they would be great grandparents, then, my thoughts shifted to Antonio...Then Kylah. I cried and cried until anger overwhelmed my emotions. I opened my eyes and saw my reflection in the water.I was unrecognizable to myself. I threw my head back and hit it on the back of the tub. I waited a moment and did it again. I repeated the action over and over until I felt nothing but dizziness. Not sadness, not remorse, not guilt... I lightly touched the back of my head with my fingertips. It filled my hands with blood. I could feel myself lose consciousness, my eyes rolled in the back of my head. I whispered "I'm sorry." Before I completely blacked out.

CHAPTER 19

I woke up to my uncle shaking me lightly, screaming at me to wake up and look at him. I began to cough and water poured from my mouth. I couldn't open my eyes. I heard EMT's gather in the bathroom and I felt the sudden warmth of clothes and a blanket being put on me. I blacked out and came to multiple different times. It was hours until I actually woke up and stayed conscious. As soon as I opened my eyes I attempted to rip the IV out my hand and get out of bed. I was disoriented and thought I was having another nightmare. When I realized I was awake, in my actual reality, I felt the worst.

"Why didn't I die?" I said crying and throwing my head into the pillow. "Why couldn't you let me die!"

I was too weak to stand. I got up and quickly fell to the ground. 3 nurses rushed in to see if I was ok. I began to throw a fit, kicking and screaming that I wanted to die. Going on and on about being alone until I felt a needle in my arm. My eyes opened slowly and I had no grasp of time. I looked around for a clack and saw that it was 4am. I overheard my dad and uncle talking to the doctor. He told them that after my 24 hour hold I'd be admitted into the psych ward. They tried to argue the doctor down, but they're allowed to admit me involuntarily. My dad tried to say it wasn't needed and that I'd be fine until the doctor read his observations. Disregarding the obvious of why I was there to begin with, my blood pressure was unusually high. While I was on a mood stabilizer, anesthetics, or simply asleep I fell into deep nightmares. He stressed that he knew they didn't spring up either. He continued down the list until he no longer wanted to hear it. I pretended to be sleep when they came in. My dad rubbed my head.

"My sunshine, why didn't you tell me you were hurting?"

I laid there still, until I actually fell asleep. I woke up the next day and had breakfast, lunch and a snack. I didn't say a word to anybody. I watched the clock until it was time for me to go to psych. I shut my eyes and imagined Antonio's touch and smell…Kylah's laugh. I pictured a time when everything was simple between us all. The first time I went over her house, I just couldn't pin point the downfall. Then I realized, there wasn't a downfall. I lost them both, at once. I was the one falling, I was the one hitting rock bottom.

I opened my eyes and immediately closed them when I felt tears stream down my face. The nurse came in and started talking to me, but I tuned her out. She laid underclothes, scrubs and shoes on my bed and left. I got up slowly and dragged myself into the bathroom. I stood in the corner to change to ensure I wouldn't catch a glimpse of myself in the mirror. I shut my eyes while I brushed my teeth, and turned off the light while I was still standing there. Walking out of the bathroom I started to feel the effect of slamming my head into the tub. My head felt heavy but my body was hollow. I couldn't even feel my heart beat in my chest. I got back in the bed and sat up, rocking myself back and forth slowly. I hummed my favorite song.

"*Lady Lover, why have you gone away. I miss you dearly, why have you gone astray. I've lost all feeling. I need to feel your touch. Oh, Lady Lover, please come back and stay.*"

I hummed the same line over and over again. My head ached and I was sensitive to every sound. I even heard the clock ticking. The time came and I was taken out the hospital in a wheel chair. I passed by my father and uncle, they looked mortified, but still ran over and hugged me, pretending to be strong.

"You should've let me die." I said under my breath.

I was on the bus with about a dozen more people. I ignored the man talking to himself, and the lady infront of me twitching and rocking. There was a boy my age, drawing or writing something in the air, so I got up sat beside him.

"What are you in for?"

"You make it seem like we're going to jail."

He laughed and shook his head.

"We are."

"Well, in that case, let's just say I lost everything all at once and I didn't really see a point for life anymore. So, because of that I threw my head into metal and let myself slip under my bath water."

He stopped tracing things into the air and looked at me, seemingly amused.

"You know, when people say 'let's just say' they usually continue with something hypothetical or vague."

"I guess. What are you in for?'"

"I'm told I have hallucinations or whatever. Dad doesn't want to deal with the fact that mom is still there. Then there's my girlfriend, I mean she was there. She talks to me. I can still feel them both. But, dad doesn't want to deal with it."

"Well hello hallucinations, I'm suicide attempt."

I reached out my arm and we shook hands. He laughed and looked me up and down. I couldn't help but notice how extremely attractive he was.

"Seriously though, I'm Asher. Asher Canton."

"I'm Kori. Kori Tucker."

We talked the whole way there. I told him about what I did to lose my boyfriend and best friend and he told me about his mom, dad and girlfriend. We talked about school and other friends, different memories. He seemed shocked about the life that I lived, I could say the same about him. We'd been on the bus for almost two hours and it seemed like we still had more road to cover.

"So, when is the last you've seen them?"

"Earlier, when we were talking. My girlfriend was here. Her name is Sade by the way. She was sitting right there in the other row, reading a book. When I seemed to be in a daze, I was staring at her, she looked up and smiled at me, winked like she always did. I looked at you and looked back at her, but she was gone. I haven't seen either since."

"Why haven't you let it go? Moved on?"

"Why haven't you?"

He replied quickly, looking deep into my eyes.

"I don't know."

He began to draw into the air again.

"What are you doing now?"

"Well, I was drawing my mother. Now I'm drawing you. I wasn't allowed to take my notebook and pencil because it 'fed into my fantasy' apparently." He stopped for a moment and looked at me. "You're extremely beautiful."

I blushed and went to respond, but I stopped when I saw a sign. "Welcome to Hill Side Psychiatric Center." Their motto was "You're okay, we just have to show you that you're okay."

I nudged Asher on the arm and told him to look. He turned around and his eyes glued to the center.

"We'll be put in the juvenile ward. I hope we see each other once we're inside. If we don't, I'll just imagine you there with me."

"I'll see you again. Don't worry."

He kissed me on the cheek before we were all taken off the bus. The Adults and teens were separated, so we stayed together until we got inside. It looked like a normal hospital, or an oversized doctor's office. They played creepy music and I was sure I'd see a nurse putting green goo into a 3-foot needle. It looked exactly how it's portrayed in movies. I began to laugh to myself. I was actually here.

They soon separated us by last name, I ended up with a 7 other people. 4 girls and 3 boys. We were all taken one by one for examination, interviews and distribution. I was the third. When I went inside I was automatically nervous, and I was still thinking about Asher.The people were asking questions they already knew the answer to. They checked me for drugs, cuts and bruises. They finger printed me, gave me a voice security code and a change of clothes, which, were worse than the scrubs. They gave me a room in the fifth ward, room 554, with a girl named Izzy Belle. I found that ironic.

I slowly walked over to the group going up the fifth floor. I looked around for Asher but I didn't see him. I stayed quiet until I got into my room. It was nice, and big. There were two seemingly comfortable beds far across from each other, a desk, and a window. It had bars, but still, a window. I went over to put the sheets they gave me on my bed. After I was done with the first layer and turned around to get the comforter, I was startled by a girl standing there, staring at me.

"Hello."

I said, backing up into my bed.

"Hello."

"Izzy?"

"Kori?"

Izzy titled her head and walked closer to me. I stood up straight and walked a few inches from my bed. She walked around me like she was judging my appearance.

"What are you doing?"

She didn't respond. After she traced my whole body she went to her bed and sat down without a word. I shrugged my shoulders and finished making my bed. After, I laid down and began to hum my favorite song. I thought about Antonio too, it was June 6th and I knew I would miss prom and graduation.After a while, I drifted to sleep, but I soon fell into a nightmare. Izzy shook me awake when I started to toss and turn. I woke up so quickly I couldn't remember what the dream was about.

"Hey Izzy."

I said in a low tone. She was standing right in front of my bed.

"Hello."

She smiled and skipped back over to her bed. I watched as she threw her legs up and down, keeping herself busy. I shook my head and got up slowly. I left the room and walked around the ward. There were a bunch of girls talking, getting along it seemed like. Maybe their illnesses didn't collide. I went into the floors' bathroom and prepared myself to look in the mirror. I took a deep breath and turned to look at myself. I didn't recognize myself still. Whoever I was looking at, looked like she needed a good night's sleep and a hug. I put my hair into a tighter bun and threw water onto my face to wake myself up. I put more pep in my step and walked over to the floors common room. I saw Asher out of the corner of my eye.

"Hey! I'm on the girls' side of the floor."

I said, walking across the room.

"I'm on the other side. My roommate is a total ass. I'll be out here as much as possible."

I went to respond when his eyes refocused onto an empty chair and he began walking away.

"Asher?"

I said, but I didn't get a response. I watched as he sat down and began talking to an empty chair. He waved me over and I walked to him with caution.

"Who is this?"

"It's my mom. Isn't she lovely?"

Said caressing the air. He really believed she was there. All of a sudden there was a bunch of commission coming from down the hall. Somebody must have been fighting or something. When we both turned back to face the chair, Asher said she was gone. He cried about how he thinks he's losing touch with them, because they don't stay for that long anymore. He grabbed my hand and told me to close my eyes and imagine Kylah or Antonio, so I did. I imagine Antonio, sitting on the bench after a game, looking up and seeing me for the first time. Asher told me to open my eyes quickly, when I did, Antonio was still sitting there, looking at me.

I jumped up and hugged him.

"Baby! I'm so glad you're here."

I looked back to see Asher smiling.

"I told you, it works."

Antonio, Asher and I talked for about an hour before we were all called back to our rooms. I walked back slowly, trying to take as much time to part from Asher. I walked into my room to see Izzy sitting on the floor facing the wall. She turned her head and nodded.

"Hello Kori."

"Hi, uh Amanda?"

She laughed.

"Yeah, who else? Don't mind me, I'm just meditating."

I rolled my eyes and laid on my bed. I closed my eyes and pictured Kylah lying next to me, doing homework and talking. I slowly opened my eyes and looked to the side. She was sitting there, beautiful as always. I just watched her and listened to her voice. Thinking about her, and having seen Antonio was tearing me apart.

CHAPTER 20

It'd been three weeks now and they called our ward over the loud speaker
for dinner, like they did every day. I watched all the kids spill out of their
rooms and gather in the café. I lagged in the back and kept my head down.
I sat in the back and scanned the room for Asher. I didn't see him like I
usually did, I got up to go into the hall way when I was approached by a
man in a suit.

"Kori Tucker?"

I backed myself into a wall and just stared at him.

"I need you to come with me."

"Why? What did I do?"

He grabbed my arm and I began to scream. All eyes turned on me and
a nurse came running up to us.

"Don't worry, I'm not going to hurt you. I'm with the police. You're not
in any trouble. Come with me."

I reluctantly began to follow him down the hall, wondering what this
could be about. Had Antonio gotten in trouble? Did Angela think I was
missing? Questions ran through my mind as I was being taken out of the
psych ward.

"Wait! Asher! I have to say bye."

"He's been taken for evaluation. You can't see him. Now let's go."

I pressed my face against the glass of the black SUV and watched as
the hospital faded in the distance. Rain drops fell from the sky one after
the other, dancing around on the window next to me. The tears streaming

down my face matched every drop. My heart felt so hollow inside my chest and I replayed every moment leading up to this. After a while I laid my head against the window and fell asleep. I dreamt about a completely different life. The one I was supposed to have with my actual parents. The dream went into a different direction. Martin and Aaron were there, but they weren't doing anything bad. They were a part of my life. Coming to birthday parties, school plays, giving me advice and rides to school.

I felt the car slowing down and I woke up after a few minutes. I was at the police station and two officers came to the back to get me. I kept my mouth closed and I walked inbehind them. I stood there and watched the officers scan their cards and talk to other officers until another guy came up and whispered something to them. The officers told me to follow them and we walked for five more minutes until we got into an interrogation room. I sat there for a while until an officer came in with a file.

"What's this about?"

"Your finger print was taken in order to be admitted into the Psychiatric hospital."

"Okay, so?"

I said, beginning to squirm in my seat.

"Cassie Powers?"

My eyes shot open and I began to stare into the officers' eyes and he stared back into mine. Detective Grayson was the cleanest cut man I ever saw. He has caramel like skin and arms that look so warm and protecting, but his eyes are different. They look as if they are darts with a target. His voice is deep, it stopped me in my tracks. His voice could stop anyone in their tracks, just like me.

"My name is Kori Tucker."

I was watching him pull out the chair that was sitting across from me, he went to sit, but didn't.

"Why am I here?"

Our eye contact was broken when he looked down at the file on the desk.

"You have no idea?" He said as he finally took a seat.

"No, I don't. Am I in some kind of trouble?"

"No. Honey I'm about to break some news to you. The real you, the you, you don't even know that you are."

My heart began to race. I know. I know full well what was happening.I began to feel heavy, but I don't want to give myself away so I answered immediately.

"I don't follow."

"Your name is Cassie Powers, your parents' names are Carson and Chasity Powers. Everyone thought you were killed in a car accident with your parents, but you were kidnapped by Martin Tucker. Luckily, but somewhat unluckily, when you were a baby your mother and father had you fingerprinted. When you were admitted into psych, which, is the unlucky part, there was an immediate red flag in the department."

The words spilled from his mouth like he tried to process it himself. It is the truth. My life was taken from me once, I undoubtedly remembered that. I just couldn't believe they are trying to take away the one I've come to know. My voice began to crack as I plead my case.

"My name is Kori Tucker. Martin Tucker is my father, my *real* father. I'd like to go home to him, please."

He knows I'm lying. I know that. I can feel the tension rising, and the elephant in the room pulling up a chair. He let out a laugh, a filler for his disbelief, and continued on.

"What did Mr. Tucker tell you about your mother?"

"My mother died at child birth."

I said forcing my burning, lying tears out of my eyes. I watched as they disappeared into the fabric of my jeans. I said it with such conviction, I began to believe myself. I began disregarding all the emotional and actual physical pain. I stopped being able to picture myself in my parents' arms. In Carson and Chasity's arms.

My heart started to feel as if it was no longer beating. Gone with my beats are the once comforting sounds of my 'could have been' mother, and the one's that returned derived from hurt.

"You know the truth butter cup, tell our story."

I heard over and over. I fought the urge to slap my hands against my ears and try to sound her out. I had to lay my head down. Detective Grayson sings a satisfied and sarcastic tune when he says

"Tired of denying?"

I listened as he left the room and slammed the door. I took a deep breath and my mind began to run wild. They can't really keep me here. I began to think about Asher, I thought I would have more time with him, he's the only one that could actually begin to understand me. I began to think about Antonio and the fact that he had no choice but to believe me now. There's no way I can get Kylah back, but I honestly needed her back. I sat there with my head dead, the inside of my stomach feels like it was letting off fireworks. I began to think about my baby and what I will do now. My mind went a million different ways and I still didn't feel my heart beat. Not once. I felt tears stream down my face but I quickly slapped them away as soon as I heard footsteps approach.

"We're going to send you to a home for girls. As soon as we put the pieces together to arrest Martin Tucker, you will be placed. I'm sorry we had to throw all this on you, we just don't need you in that toxic environment. Look where that landed you."

Detective Grayson smirked harder with every word. I decided not to say anything. We drove twenty minutes out of town before we came to a complete stop infront of a beaten up, bar windowed home for girls. I stared into the rearview mirror in hopes Grayson would see the fear in my eyes and not take me in, but he couldn't look back anyway. I waited for another officer to open my door and began to scan the area before I went in. I immediately heard catty girls arguing in the back and a faint smell of piss and caught a glimpse of dry blood. I avoided eye contact after I rolled my eyes at the lady sitting at the front desk, popping gum and rolling stiff weave in here fingers. I took three steps behind the officer as he told her the information. I began to look around and kept making eye contact with every girl walking by.

The officer turned me loose and I immediately blocked myself into a corner. I heard a constant whisper from a distance so I peeked around the corner to see what it was. A girl that I couldn't quote make out waved me over and disappeared into a room. I proceeded with caution as I tried to go unnoticed. I began to look around to see where she was when I felt a slight tug on the arm. My head snapped back and I followed the fast moving shadow into another blocked off corner. Before I got any closer I had to ball my fist.

"What do you want?"

"You know around here our first conversation is an introduction." The girl replied with a deep southern accent. I scoffed and un-balled my fist.

"I'm not going to repeat myself."

"Why are you standing here in front of me, pageant girl?"

"You don't know me."

"I know you don't belong."

She let of a subtle dangerous vibe. Her skin reminded me of a fudge

I'd love to indulge and I couldn't get over how deep her eyes are. I wasn't trying to stare but I was. Her slender body seemed to go on and on and I can't get over how deep her eyes are. I took a step forward,

"So what?"

"You have anybody to go home to?" She said as she pulled a box down from the shelf across the room.

"Yeah, I do." I said with confusion.

"Then home you shall go."

A smirk planted across her face and she began to move swiftly. I hesitated before following her every step.

"Where are we-."

"Hush!"

She said as she sharply turned her head to look at me. We got to the corner of a hallway when she stopped and took a few steps backwards.

"I'm going to distract our guard, there's a blind spot by that door, keep running straight until you hit Gatemen, it's a side street, from there, you're on your own. RUN!"

I watched her rush across the room and attack some girl that was sitting there. As soon as I saw the security leave her post I ran, and kept on running. There was a break in the fence surrounding the building, I carefully slid under and continued to run. When I hit the side street, I stopped running and took a breather. I looked around the rural area and began to walk slowly down the street, trying my best to observe my surroundings. I was surprised that such an uppity neighborhood would be around a home for girls.

I was walking for a few moments until I was stopped by a boy sitting on the stairs smoking.

"Come here ma."

I started to ignore him but changed my mind, there was a car parked in front and I wanted to take my best chances at getting home.

"You lost?"

"Yeah actually, I am."

I couldn't help but make direct contact, his eyes were deep as an ocean with just the right amount of a reflecting moon. His pearly white teeth broke the dark chocolate fountain illusion that his skin let off. My mind quickly shifted off into thinking of his lips touching mine, but the thought was cut short when he began to talk again.

"Well, I can take you where you need to go."

"How do I know you're not a killer?"

"You don't."

He said as he got up and walked down the stairs. I was completely taken by surprise when I realized how tall he was.

"What's your name?"

"CJ. What's yours?"

"Kori."

"Well Kori, you look like you need a good meal and a nap. Come on."

He said as he waved me inside the house. I proceeded with caution but I didn't feel threatened. He had a simple one floor lay out, black and red interior, typical guy things everywhere.t

"You live alone?"

"Yeah, just me and my dog Biggy."

He called him into the room and the dog came running. Biggy was an understatement.

"So what are you going to feed me?'

"Whatever you want. You have to tell me what's up with you though."

"Deal."

He grabbed his keys off the counter and drove for about an hour into the city. We talked and I tried to stay within reason for details without being vague. He told me a little bit about himself, and was really nice and more than met the eyes, even though, what did meet the eye was pure perfection.

"You're really sexy."

Slipped out of my mouth in the middle of his sentence. He began to laugh and shake his head.

"Thanks."

"That's it?"

"What you want? For me to tell you you're the hottest girl I've ever seen?"

I blushed and rolled my eyes at the same time. I looked out the window and something triggered in my head.

"Where are you going?"

"This restaurant called cravings."

My heart began to beat out my chest.

"This uh. This is exactly um, where I need to uh- be."

"Are you ok?"

He said, slowing the car down.

"Just a lot of thoughts I can't really turn off."

"If you need to go I understand, I'll just pick up your food and drop you off."

I started to shake my head and try to calm myself down. We got food and I told him to drop me off in front of Antonio's house.

"Nice to meet you Kori. Call me if you ever want to do this again."

I took his number down and blew him a kiss before running to the house, trying to go unseen. I knocked softly and his dad came to the door.

"Kori."

"Is Antonio here?"

"Yeah, I'll get him."

He began to call his name but I cut him off.

"No, don't. I'll just go up."

"I don't think you want to do that honey."

I pushed through him and ran up the stairs. I slowly cracked his door to see him having sex with someone else. I burst through the door and he quickly pushed her off of him.

"Kori! What the hell!"

I watched as the girl pulled the cover over her naked body and ran to the bathroom.

"Baby I can... Wait, what am I doing?" He said putting on his shorts. "Get out!"

I began to break down crying and fell to the floor. Antonio ran to my side.

"Kori? What? What is it?"

"Please, I need you. Don't push me away. I am so sorry. Let me explain everything."

"Wha-. Where have you been?"

I began to cry harder and he lifted me up and put me on the bed. He went into the bathroom and escorted the girl out. When he came back in he sat far away from me.

"Start at the beginning."

CHAPTER 21

He sat across the room. I watched him look back at me, expecting to see anger, but all I saw was hurt and a blend of curiosity.

"Antonio, I just want to say I am so-."

He put his hand up to stop me from continuing on. He knew I was going to apologize.

"I said start from the beginning Kori. I don't want to hear anything else."

My heart began to race. I knew this was the very moment I could get him back or lose him forever.

"Nothing I know about myself is true. Not my name, not my father, not my uncle... Nothing."

"So fucking vague Kori."

Antonio said getting up, I could see his heart falling deeper inside himself.

"Ok...I'll start from the begging." I said shifting on the bed, watching him pace. "Martin had a mental breakdown after his girlfriend lost their baby. Then he started talking to Aaron about him seeing me, and I guess they both agreed to kidnap me."

Antonio scoffed and sat back down.

"They killed my parents Antonio. They caused us to get into a car accident, took me out of the car and set it on fire. Fast forward a few years and here I am. Kori Tucker. Back in the beginning of the school year I went searching around the house and found a death certificate, I thought it was my mother's but it was Martin's old girlfriend, he killed her. When I came to your house that night and April was singing 'I'm a little tea cup' I had continuous nightmares about the accident. When I told my dad about it he started acting all weird, worse than usual. I would hear conversations between Aaron and Martin that helped me put pieces together, but then there was Angela. She came to get me from school and told me how she was best friends with my parents, and how she thought I as dead until she saw me with Martin, she trusted her gut and came into my life to try to take him down."

"Angela? Kylah's Angela?"

He said in disbelief, but continued to listen.

"We've been gathering information that they kept in the extra room we have in the house. That's when all the pieces of the puzzle began to fall together."

"So who are these mystery parents?"

"Well, when Kylah and I got the 'pick your tragedy' assignment I'd told her about the nightmares, so we looked up the tragedy that fit the description... Carson and Chasity Powers."

Antonio's head snapped to the side. He pulled out his phone and began typing something, waited for a moment, and did something again. A few moments later He dropped to his knees and crawled over to me.

"I am so sorry. I am so sorry I didn't believe you."

I began to say something but he continued.

"This doesn't explain where you've been."

"Well... After we broke up, Kylah came over and we broke up too. She hated me, you hated me. My father wasn't my father and I wasn't myself and I hit my head. On purpose, repeatedly."

He remained on his knees and held my legs tighter.

"I was transported from the hospital to a mental facility and I was fingerprinted, that's how the police found me. They questioned me, but they already knew everything. They took me to a home and left me there, saying I would be placed when they had all the evidence to convict Martin and Aaron."

I pulled him up and made him look me in my eyes.

"That's why we have to go."

"Go?"

"We need to get out of here baby. We have a baby, you won't see me again if I'm placed, who knows what will happen our kid. I don't want to lose you. I don't want to lose anybody."

Antonio looked away and took a few steps back.

"Martin and Aaron? You still care about them after what they did to you?"

"No matter what they did they kept me safe for all this time this is the least I can do for them."

"The least? You don't owe them anything! Especially Martin, did you forget all the times he beat you?"

"I do. I owe them because I met you."

He scoffed and slapped his hands on his face, turned quickly and went into the closet. I watched him throw thousands of dollars in a bag, a few of his favorite clothes and mine that I left.

"You're helping me? Coming with me? After all that has happened?"

"I'm your ride or die, like you've always been to me. Now grab some bags, we're going to Curry's. I'm sure he'll be glad to see you."

We quickly gathered our things into the car and pulled off. I pressed my face to the window like I was a kid pulling up to the circus. I rolled the window down slightly so I could smell the air. It hit my nose like I'd had a cold for months and was finally able to breathe. All the love and pain that I've gone through here was replaying over and over in my head. I felt the baby forming inside me, like she was popping bubbles in my stomach.

"I think it's a girl."

I said rubbing my stomach, turning to look at Antonio.

"What?"

"I think it's a girl."

"Really?"

He said, not even turning the slightest bit to look at me. He seemed to have detective Grayson's targeted eyes as he turned onto Curry's street. Walking into Curry's it seemed like more security than usual. Like always we went straight back into his office and a sinister smile slipped onto his face.

"Robin! Here I go thinking Skinner here killed you after he found out about you taking me up on our little deal."

I looked over to Antonio and watched emptiness fill his eyes.

"I need your help."

"I'm going to need a little bit more information than that Skinner.

Most people asking for help are asking for money and you are my best paid hitter."

"I'm not asking for money. I'm asking for help."

I quickly cut in.

"I need help Curry. My family and our unborn child."

Curry dismissed his security detail but I could still feel the heaviness of their presence. I began to explain as much as I could before I got lost in my story. Curry took out a note pad and pen and began writing something down. He slid it across the desk.

"I got you a house 2 hours out of town, in 4 days somebody will be knocking at your doors with new identities a new house with a nursery and everything. I'll have some information given to you in regards of school and everything else."

I ran around to the desk and hugged him. He told us to hurry and I grabbed the note, and turned to leave. Before my hand touched the door knob he spoke again.

"You have to leave this life behind you Robin. You have to leave yourself and take on a new identity. A conscience one. You can't look back."

Antonio and I looked at him in silence and waited moments until he continued.

"You too Skinner. The only person you know is me. I can arrange you seeing April but that's it. Say your goodbye's, keep it short, sweet and vague. If you two get caught, I get caught. I'll know before the police and I'm ruthless when it comes to myself."

Antonio squeezed my hand tighter. My body was so numb I didn't feel him grab it.

"One more thing." He continued. "Pick your names."

"Morgan."

Antonio said quickly.

"Karley."

Curry smiled and dismissed us. We walked slowly back into the car and sat there, silent. I felt tears stream down my face.

"You don't have to do this."

"Yes I do. I've graduated, I needed to move out anyways. I'll see my family again." Antonio rubbed his head and continued. "It needs to just be us. Warn your folks or whatever you have to do, but we need to be gone by sun down."

"Take me to my fathers."

Antonio shook his head but pulled off without a word and the ride there continued that way. I hesitated to get out of the car, having debilitating flash backs as I scanned my surroundings. I walked quickly to the door and began to knock rapidly but the door was already opened. I walked in to see the house the same and empty at the same time. There was no sign of life. The couches weren't sat on, the tv stood still, unwatched.

"Dad? Uncle Sandy?"

I said softly as I walked upstairs. It was cold, the air felt like it was leaving cuts in my skin. I walked into Martin's room with caution. The bed was made, nothing was out of place. Nothing. I swiftly walked into my room. Nothing was out of place. Nothing. I ran to all my hiding places and everything was gone. I put everything back in its place. I couldn't feel my heart inside my chest. I swiftly moved to the extra room. The padlock was off and it was cracked the tiniest bit. I pushed the door open and slid inside. It was empty. Not even an outline of the boxes that sat on the floor were there. My mind went blank and I turned around slowly. Walking towards the door there was a sign taped onto the back.

"We loved you and I'm sorry."

I snatched the note off the wall and ran down the stairs back into the car.

"There's nothing for me here."

Antonio started to say something but stopped and pulled off. I slapped tears off of my face before they could fall. I was thinking about everything, but somehow nothing. A few moments later we pulled up to Chase's house and Kylah was sitting on the porch, looking good as always. She rolled her eyes and got up to go in the door. I jumped out the car before it came to a complete stop and ran after her.

"Please!"

I screamed out, grazing her arm.

"Please what? Please be heart-broken but pretend not to be? Fuck you Kori. Like I said."

"I'm sorry. I'm so sorry."

"Sorry? Sorry isn't going to cut it. You weren't sorry when you kissed me and made my heart leap out of my chest for your own amusement. You weren't sorry when you took me to Snow's. You want Antonio, remember? He's right there. Go get him."

I grabbed Kylah, and hugged her tightly, ignoring her struggling.

"I love you. I'm sorry."

She stopped fighting and broke down in my arms.

"I love you...I love you too."

"I won't see you for a long time Kylah. Don't forget me. I'll see you, I promise."

I turned around to leave when she grabbed me.

"They found out?"

"Tell Angela I'm sorry. I couldn't be strong."

Kylah shook her head and I watched as she sunk deep within herself. She pushed my hair back and kissed me deeply and then softly once again. She held out her pinky.

"Promise if we never see each other again, you won't forget me. Promise your baby will know me."

I intertwined my pinky with hers.

"Pinky Swear."

I hugged her one last time and ran back to the car. I knew Antonio was watching but he didn't say anything about it.

"You ready?"

I shook my head and stopped myself from looking back. I laid my hand on my stomach and closed my eyes. I heard Antonio turn on the radio and tap the steering wheel. He rapped for at least an hour before he turned off his music and asked me if I wanted food.

I didn't recognize the area even though we didn't go that far. I watched people walk around, ride bikes and gather around on the porch. People lived here. People made lives here. Antonio pulled up to some knock off cravings that was packed to only be 7 at night.

"I don't want to go in."

"Well they have take-out."

"I'm not hungry."

"Well get hungry."

"What's your problem Antonio?"

He got out the car and slammed the door. I saw him say something but I couldn't make it out. I got out the car after him and he slammed me onto the driver's side.

"Get back in the car Kori."

Fear struck my eyes but I didn't see anger in Antonio's. I saw hurt and worry.

"What's wrong?"

"I need you to work with me Ko…Karley. We need to start a new life and I'm trying. Please, work with me."

I shook my head and followed him into the restaurant. We got food and about an hour and a half later we got to the house Curry set up for us. As soon as we walked in the lights cut on automatically, lighting up each room perfectly. It's laid with hardwood floors and white circular rugs, and right in the middle of it all was a gold fountain. All three living rooms were connected by a huge window that had a view to the pool.

"Curry had this in his back pocket?

I said in amazement, Following the paintings on the wall. I soon found myself in front of a spiral staircase. Walking slowly up the stairs with Antonio following close behind my eyes widened to see what was behind the giant brown doors. Taking Antonio's hand ad pushing it open we walked in together. The room was a giant, laid with grey and gold furniture. Televisions were inside of the wall and floating about the bed, which, had a glass door to close it off from everything else. There was an electronic fireplace and a view into the city. It was beautiful.

"If this is what he put us in for a few days, imagine what the house we're going to live in will look like."

I turned to Antonio and stared at him.

"What?"

"Let's tear this room up."

A sinister smile took over Antonio's face and he ran over to me like I had the world in my hands. He looked at me as if it was our first time all over again. He made sure to be gentle though, and every chance he got he would kiss my stomach and tell me he loved me. We kept going for hours, in every room. When we noticed it getting lighter we sat in front of the giant window casting over the city and held each other.

"Morgan." I said, looking up to him, still laying on his bare chest. "I love you."

"I love you too. Way too much…"

We spent the next three days disregarding the problems that we had faced and decided to leave the past in the past. We anticipated Curry's arrival and looked up for the future, hoping, of course, everything went smoothly.

CHAPTER 22

The visit came July 15th, 2003. I was in the kitchen about to cook breakfast when we heard a knock on the door. Antonio grabbed his gun and opened it with caution. Three guys walked in before Curry, two arming the door and one right by his side.

"Batman and Robin. How you liking the place?"

"It's great."

I said in hopes of lifting the tension.

"What you got for us?"

"Well, I take it yawl haven't watched the news."

We shook our heads and followed him into one of the living rooms. He turned on the tv, sat down and watched. My face was plastered on the news. They thought Martin and Aaron had stolen me from the girls' home and ran off with me again. It was a 20,000-dollar award for leading information on them. They raved about this on every different channel. There were rumors on the famous 'Gossip All The Time' show that there was going to be a movie about us.

"We're going to need to change your look baby."

Curry said as he signaled one of his guards. They left the house, returning with some fashion guru type lady.

"I'm going to make you look fantastic darling."

Antonio and Curry went in the other room and left me there to have my identity take a 360 degree turn. She dyed my hair red at the roots and blonde all the way through to make me look like a red head whom died her hair blonde. She got some tattoo simulator to give me a beauty mark above my lip, on the side of my face just below my ear, and under my eye on top of my cheek bone. After she was done she shaved off a few inches from my hair and gave me a lip injection. After she way done her face lightened up and she stop being tense. She told me to get up and followed me into the bathroom to look at myself.

"Just as beautiful, just different. Aye?"

She said looking at me as if she made me from scratch.

"I just hope Antonio liked it."

I whispered to myself, touching my lips and putting my hair into different styles.

"I need to set you up with baby vitamins, doctors and other information now."

The lady put on glasses and pulled out a suitcase. She had all prenatal vitamins I would need for the next 6 and a half months. I had my own private doctor, and would have a private teacher for the rest of high school. She took my picture and printed out my new identity. Just like that I was Karley Harrison. She gave me a new phone, a card with 5,000 dollars on it and another 5 in cash. She told me the rules too and I could tell they came straight from Curry.

- No connections with the past.
- Don't blow all the money all at once.
- Don't cause any unneeded attention.
- The only time you contact somebody of importance is through me.
- Try to fit in, but keep relationships at a minimum,
- Don't forget I own you and you owe me.
- Don't try to handle anything on your own.
- Notify me and me only if you feel compromised or in danger.
- Don't ask questions. Everything is on a 'need to know' basis.
- You fuck up, you die.

There was a copy for me to keep and a copy for me to sign. I stared at the paper for 3 minutes before I could bring myself to move my hand. I finally signed it and shook with every cursive letter. I signed Karley Harrison. Kori Tucker is dead. Karley Harrison is a 20-year-old from Cincinnati. My parents died when I was 15 and I got sent to live with my grandmother in Allentown, Florida. When she got sick I moved her into a nursing home and that's where I met my boyfriend. 22-year-old Morgan Flint. Simple as that and end of story.

The effects of the dose mixed with morning sickness and fear overwhelmed my body. While Antonio and Curry continued to talk business I went to sleep. I didn't think and I didn't dream. Three hours went by before I was being lifted of the bed and placed in a car. I heard faint voices and the brunt force of the air hitting my skin when the bags were placed in the car and the doors were slammed.

I opened my eyes as the car pulled off and stared at the part of Antonio's face I could see. He was serious but didn't look stressed or worried. Curry was in the passenger seat. They didn't talk, they both just looked straight ahead. I couldn't keep my eyes open. I woke up seemingly hours later when I felt the car stop. When I peeked out the window I noticed there was nothing around. Nothing. It was one of those towns where everybody was there for the viewing of everyone's birth. The type of town with secrets smart people wouldn't try to uncover. It was just a pit stop though, so I hoped we were just passing by.

"Get up."

Antonio said, throwing his hand to the back, shaking my leg. I got up slowly and caught a glimpse of myself, Karley really, in the mirror. I rubbed my face and stretched.

"Where are we?"

"Outskirts of Allentown baby, right on the border of our new lives."

Curry grunted and got out of the car. We both sat there for a few seconds before he hit the window and told us to come on. When we got out the car I noticed Antonio's bleeding knuckles and a swollen cheek.

"Baby, what happened?"

I didn't have to ask. I knew the answer. I knew that look. A smirk was appeared for a second as he looked down at his hand.

"I owe him."

He said without even looking up. *What a way to start our new lives*, I thought. We walked in the rest-stop and sat down at the table to eat.

"So Robin." Curry said, breaking the silence. "What are you going to do for me?"

"What do you want?'"

He laughed and clapped, looking at Antonio. He was not looking back at him.

"Let me ask you something. What's something someone would fight hardest for?"

"Their life."

"Their life! Yes! So, since I'm giving you and your baby life, what does that mean?"

"This is something I want to fight for? You want me to fight?"

I said confused, Antonio was still looking deeply into his plate.

"Oh, no Robin. I don't want you to fight. I want you to be smart. If it gets to the point where you have to fight, well, you weren't being too smart."

"I don't understand."

"Antonio just took the life out of somebody with his bare hands. That would be him, being smart. Now you, with child and all, I just need you to do something simple."

Antonio finally looked up and began to stare at Curry.

"Turn my profit, keep the books. Keep your ears open and watch."

"So, what? You want me to be some type of spy, project manager?"

"I want you to pick who lives and who dies. I want you to make sure my books are right. You'll be sending your boy on missions and keeping my money right. I can't be running up here every time something is wrong. I'll be mailing you shit and telling you what's up. One of my men will keep you connected."

I didn't know what to say. This all seemed to be news to Antonio.

"You putting my girl in your place? Why can't I do it?"

Curry punched him in the mouth and he fell out of his chair, leaving a splatter of blood on the table.

"Get up boy."

Curry said looking down on him. I went to get up and help when he cocked his gun under the table. Antonio wiped his mouth and spit into the napkin.

"That's why." Curry said, wiping off his rings. "Anyways, you'll be getting a car and a second phone."

He dropped the keys, phone and a stack of files in front of me. He slid Antonio a piece of paper and finished his sandwich in three bites. He dismissed us and we scrambled to the bathroom to get a wet cloth so we could leave.

Antonio handed me the paper with the address and got into the backseat without a word and laid his head down. I was so glad he taught me to drive because I don't know what I would've done. In less than 45 minutes

I was pulling up to a cabin like condo. It fit it to the "neighborhood" but you could tell it was very expensive and decked out. I was amazed at the perfectly crafted walls and high ceilings. It was perfect.

I walked slowly up the long stair case, observing every corner of the house, admiring how the room flowed together and all the doors that lead into other parts of the house. I took a glance out of a window on the side of the stairs and saw a beautiful lake and garden out back. It had giant rocks, fish and a huge patio to sit and observe. By the time I got to the second floor I was already sold. I went directly into the nursery. My jaw dropped, the room was a regular sized apartment. It had everything from the biggest basinet you could imagine to a full wall of bears and books. It was a unisex room since we didn't know what it was but it was beautiful regardless. It had glow in the dark stars hanging from the ceilings.

Antonio came in the room after a while and held me.

"We're really doing this."

"We are, Morgan."

He held his hands over my stomach as we walked together and sat on top of the giant bean bag chair.

"Let's think of some names baby."

"Antonio if it's a boy, I want a part of me to live on even if I can't be myself."

"Kylah if it's a girl... Cassie was taken from me and Kori was given, then taken. I want some type of reminder."

Antonio went to respond when we heard the thunder roll in. Rain began to poor down and shake the house. Antonio and I went to the living room and sat by the fire in silence. Antonio fell asleep and I slipped from under him. I began to look through the files and hundreds of interactions. Curry had a ridiculously large business. I continued to flip through the pages and I came across Antonio's records. He killed 13 people while I was gone. That put his count at 23. I couldn't help but think about what I released inside of him. Then I forgot that he was this monster when I met him. Now, I was in charge of who he hurt, who he killed, who he took away. I was playing with fire.

Lightning struck again and I jumped up, locking the windows and closing the curtains. I went back and continued to flip through the pages. I was shocked when I saw the guy that drove me home. He was one of the most profitable dealers. I moved over to the red file.

"Chase!"

I said aloud, waking Antonio up.

"What? What happened?"

Antonio grabbed a gun out of his pants and ran to me.

"No! Antonio… It's Chase. I think this is why Curry wanted me to do this. Chase is on his hit list."

"What? Let me see."

He snatched the file away from me. After a few moments he went crazy. He threw the file against the table and screamed louder than the rain. He punched the air and screamed again.

"What the fuck! Are you serious? This is what he wanted, he planned this shit! He knew it would hurt more coming from you. Go upstairs Kori."

"W-why? Why do I have to go?"

He got into my face and pushed me.

"GO UPSTAIRS! FOR ONCE LISTEN TO ME!"

The words rolled off his tongue like bullets. I backed all the way up into the railing, holding eye contact. He threw his hand up dismissing me. I ran to the room but slowly sat at the edge of the stairs to see what he was doing.

"I need to speak to Curry."

Antonio said in a stern voice. It took a while before Curry was brought to the phone.

"Are you fucking serious Curry? CHASE? He's not a threat to anyone! You could easily cut him off. Is this you twisted way of an I owe you? My best friend! That's why you put Kori on this? So it'll hurt more when I take the life of her best friend's boyfriend, knowing she can't be there to comfort her."

I couldn't tell what Curry was saying, but it couldn't have been good. It never was.

"No! I'm going to finish the job. I just don't understand why you have to be so vindictive. No I know I owe you. Damn it Curry. He's my friend but I need to keep Kori and my baby safe."

I felt my heart break in two. 'Finish the job'? He really made it seem like a business deal. Antonio told Curry he would be ready when he got here tomorrow. When I heard the phone hit the floor I ran back into the master bedroom. Antonio ran up the stairs and closed the door.

"Come here Kori."

I went towards him with caution. He pulled me closer and pressed his lips to my ear.

"I'm going to kill Curry."

"What?" I said pushing him away from me. "You-you can't! What will we do then?"

He pulled me back over to him.

"Come here! He could have this place bugged. Don't worry, he insisted that he come with me to kill Chase because he thought I wouldn't. I'm going to plan it perfectly and take over. Everyone respects me there and none of them will want to take power. Then, we won't owe anybody, I won't have to kill anybody and we'll have unlimited money. Plus, this is all I know."

"Do you really think you could pull it off?"

I whispered, I couldn't hear myself over my heart beat.

"He's not going to tell anybody where he's going because he never knows if one of his dudes is a mole. When we're at Chase's, I'm going to have to act like I'm going to kill him because during the ride over there is when he'll be on defense."

"But what if Kylah is there? What if he kills her so you can get right to your job?"

"I'll have to think of something. I promise I won't let her die."

"I don't know about this Antonio."

"Damn it Kori! It's that or I kill Chase."

I paced around the room and weighed every possible outcome.

"What if he kills you Antonio? What would I do then? It's not like we were ever going to see Chase again..."

"It's not like we'll ever see him again?" Antonio said. I could see his anger rising. "What happened to you Kori? You're talking like you could kill him yourself! Like he was just some guy in your math class."

"I have a baby to worry about! We need you."

"I got this Kori. Don't worry about anything. When this is over, you'll have more than you can handle."

"You don't even care about killing Curry?"

Antonio sat on the bed and threw his face into his hands.

"I would, but he's just done too much..."

He moved back onto the double king sized bed and laid down. I took off my shirt and looked into the mirror that was built into the wall.

"Look baby. I'm getting big."

Antonio got right up and glided over to me.

"You're still beautiful." He said kissing my stomach between every word. "We'll be able to tell if it's a boy or a girl now, you're already 5 months."

That moment was the first time I actually stood there and felt the baby move and kick. Tears came to Antonio's eyes.

"I love you so much already baby. Whatever you are. Daddies going to take good care of you and mommy forever."

We fantasized our baby's arrival, what he or she would look like. We talked about how it would be once Antonio was in Curry's position. We wondered what would happen if we ever ran into anybody from our past, if they'd even recognize us. We argued over bed times and when they were allowed to date, who would be the cool parent and who would always lay down the law. We established Antonio would cook and clean while I went to school and took care of the baby. I didn't know what I wanted to be, but I knew I was going.

I fell asleep in the middle of conversation and woke up a few hours later. It was 4 in the morning and Antonio seemed like he hadn't closed his eyes to blink. He was pacing back and forth and talking himself. I continued to lay there and listen. He was trying to think of the perfect plan to kill Curry, Going over every possible outcome. He stopped and grabbed a duffel bag out of our apartment sized walk in closet. He took out pinky rings, watches and earrings. He began to cry and say sorry over and over again. He took out piles of cash and put the jewelry on top of each stack.

"Your lives were priceless. I never spent the money Curry thought you were worth. I'm sorry, I'm so sorry."

He just kept repeating it over and over again. He took out a gun that was on the inside pocket of the duffel bag and put it to his head. I jumped out of bed and ran to him.

"What are you doing! No baby, please don't do this."

"Why did I get to live after all these years? All the people whose lives I took because Curry told me to jump and I said how high. He has to die. It has to stop."

He put the gun down and slapped the tears from his face. I looked at him in shock, I'd never seen him that fragile.

"Are these trophies?"

I went to grab one of the rings and he grabbed my wrist.

"Don't touch it." He said throwing my hand away. "This one was my first. The one Kevin let me kill. I felt so good. I was breathing and he wasn't...Kevin was so proud. I took his pinky ring when Kevin wasn't looking. Been collecting little shit since I started. I can't remember his name though."

He took off one of his chains and stared at it.

"She was my favorite. She looked so innocent, but she was a fighter and was deep in the game. I never really asked why he was killing her. I doubt she owed money or was trying to take over the game. She didn't show me fear. She talked to me while I was loading the gun. Her name was Michelle. People called her Bitty."

He laughed and put the necklace inside the bag. I watched him without a word.

"This guy was my sixth. He had a daughter that ran into the room right as I snapped his neck. She was 4, I wonder if she remembers me. I took his golden dog tags with her face in it." He said opening it and putting it in front of me. "Isn't she beautiful?"

"Baby."

I said reaching for his hand. He moved farther away.

"You must think I'm some pussy. I'm crying over a life that I chose. Keeping their things, remembering names. I'm torturing myself, aren't I?"

He threw everything back into the bag and placed it into the closet. I grabbed his arm before he could snatch away and pulled him to the bed. I listened to him ramble on about how he shouldn't feel the way he does and how it'll feel when he gets power. He contradicted his every statement and changed emotions ever so often.

I knew he didn't need anything but open ears. He fell asleep talking this time and I was left awake. I watched the sunrise and slid out of bed to make him breakfast. Curry came before Antonio woke up so I had to talk to him like I didn't know he was going to die today.

"Who knew you could cook Robin. How you liking your new position?"

I couldn't help but ask about the guy that drove me home.

"How long CJ been working for you?"

"You know him?"

"I know of him."

He laughed and took a few more bites of his food.

"You fuck him?"

"Oh, gosh no, why would you say that?"

"Well that's good, I was thinking about sending him down here for you to meet. You'll have a friend."

I sat there twirling my fork on the plate. Trying to hold my tongue but I couldn't.

"Why are you here?"

"We both know the answer to that Robin."

"Why are you going to kill Chase? He would be so easily taken down Curry."

He pulled his chair closer to me and gulped down his orange juice.

"To see Skinner do it."

He laughed and stood up, pulling a stack out his pocket.

"What do I have to do for this?"

"You gave me breakfast Robin. Calm down. Not everything is a game."

"Yes it is!" I said slamming my hand on the table. "That's all it is. Did you hear what you just said?"

Curry walked back up to me, keeping eye contact the entire time.

"Well baby, I love to play."

He went in for a kiss and I pushed him away, backing into the counter. He pulled my hair so hard I heard my neck crack as he pushed himself against me.

"Please don't do this." I begged, digging my nails into his arms, struggling to free myself from his grip.

"What's something someone will fight their hardest for?"

Antonio said as he appeared behind him, holding the gun to Curry's head.

"Their life. So are you going to fight Curry? For your life?"

Curry reached for his gun and Antonio took the safety off.

"You'll be dead before you can pull it."

He let me go and I ran across the room.

"You're crossing the line Skinner."

"Fuck you!"

Antonio said right before he spat in Curry's face.

"Get on the floor."

"You have got to be out your mind boy. I'm not getting on shit. You going to have to kill me."

"Oh, I plan to."

"And do what? Take over? I made you. Look what I gave to you. You-."

"I what? I owe you? I took a house you never use so you give my girl the biggest hand in your business? So you make me kill my best friend? What were you going to do to Kori? Huh? Wanted to fucking play? Well

I'm not playing anymore! We got ambushed and you got hit, asked me to put you out your misery. I did, your boys know who I am. I'll have everyone behind me."

Curry began to scream on the top of his lungs.

"I BUILT THIS SHIT FROM THE GROUND UP! HOW DARE YOU! I GAVE YOU EVERY-."

Antonio put a bullet right between his eyes. The ring of the shot danced through the air. He stood there with a blank but confused stare. I walked over slowly and took the gun out of his hands.

"It's over baby." I said grabbing his face. "It's over."

CHAPTER 23

"Are you ok baby? Did he hurt you?"

Antonio said dropping to his knees, pulling closer to me. He kissed my stomach and grabbed my butt.

"Mm. Baby, I'm the plug now. I'm about to give you the world."

"How are we going to get him out of here? Do you really think everybody will fall in line?"

"Don't worry about that. Everybody knew if something was to happen I would be the heir. You're right though, I do need help with his body. Can you go grab plastic wrap out the kitchen? You know anybody that would help?"

I immediately began to think about CJ.

"Yeah, I got someone."

I went upstairs while Antonio cleaned the blood and called CJ.

"What's up? Who this?"

"It's Kori. What's up stranger?"

He laughed and shuffled around.

"What you want, trouble?"

"So baby I know a little bit more about you than you think. You got a little track record with Curry."

He coughed and adjusted the phone.

"What!?

"I'm at 5658 Burk wood in Allentown. I need you to come to see me."

"Damn girl. You are something else."

"So are you coming?"

"I'm on my way."

I went to turn around and go back downstairs but Antonio was already in the doorway.

"Who was that?"

"The guy that took me home. He was in one of Curry's files so I decided to call him, I knew he'd help if-."

"If what? If it was you asking?"

My heart raced as he moved closer to me. I fell into the chair sitting on the side of the room.

"No it's not like that, he's just the only one out here."

"Word? What does he look like?"

I tried to keep a straight face, but remembering his dark chocolate complexion, perfect teeth and deep eyes took over me. I smiled and looked away for a second, and snapped right back.

"I uh, I don't, I don't know he's just a regular guy I- I guess."

Antonio lifted me by my arms and threw me back into a wall.

"Get that fucking smile off your face." He said, lifting me off my feet. "Is this nigga gone be a problem?"

My face was struck with fear.

"No baby. Please, you're hurting me, put me down."

He let me down onto the floor but kept me pinned against the wall.

"I'm going to be watching the both of yawl. I promise you I will blow his brains out and make you clean it up." He said releasing one of my arms to punch the wall. "I'll be damned if you hurt me again."

He slammed me against the wall one last time before he let me go.

"When he calls you, give me the phone. You got me?"

I shook my head rapidly. I kept my eyes pinned to the floor, I couldn't look at him.

"Now sit your ass down."

I sat on the bed for 25 minutes anticipating the call, then it came. I ran downstairs and handed the phone to Antonio.

"Yo baby I'm outside."

I could hear the words fall from his mouth a seep through the phone. I sunk deep into myself as I watched Antonio turn around.

"Baby?"

He said grabbing the back of my neck, pushing me to open the door.

I opened it and there he was, sexy. I fought back a smile as he hugged me. As soon as he saw Antonio he pulled out his gun.

"What the fuck is going on."

I turned around to see Antonio pulling his gun out.

"What's up nigga?"

"Kori, you set me up?"

"No, no. Please can you both put your guns down. This is not what this is CJ. Antonio, stop it!"

They both put their guns down with caution, eye balling each other.

"CJ, this is Antonio, my boyfriend."

"And her baby father." Antonio said walking closer to us. "What the fuck is up with you, nigga?"

CJ ignored Antonio and looked at me confused.

"What am I doing here? And why are you a blonde?"

I pulled him deeper into the house and shut the door. I pointed at Curry and Cj stepped back.

"We can't lift him alone."

"You did that, trouble?"

"Nah."

I said shaking my head, watching CJ pull his sleeves up.

"What am I getting out of this?"

"You can keep your life."

CJ laughed and scoffed.

"Who's life you threatening? Nigga I don't know who you are and you're not intimidating. I got guns with bullets to. Get over yourself."

I was surprised at CJ's response but honestly didn't expect any different. Antonio looked shocked.

"Why you calling her baby?"

"Man I call every girl baby. Yo feelings hurt, Pussy? You got a dead body on the floor and you worried about who calling your girl baby? I don't want her, man, she just a cool ass girl."

CJ began to laugh and I waited for Antonio to get mad and yell but he didn't.

"Man I'm not a pussy. And alright, she said you was just a friend."

"Word? Here I go thinking she wanted me."

"Stop it!" I said, jokingly slapping his arm. "Can you help us or not?"

"Yeah baby. Let's go Toni, or whatever the fuck your name was. Quicker we get this body, the quicker I can spark up."

I was relieved once the tension in the room lifted. Antonio and CJ were talking to each other. It was so weird how boys started 'friendships' or whatever it was going to be. They got everything cleaned up and CJ went into town with Antonio.

I was alone for a few hours before my baby's doctor came to the door. We were going to find out the sex of the baby. We made small talk as she set up her equipment. I couldn't hide my excitement. After she checked to make sure nothing was physically wrong with the baby she said it was a girl. We were having a girl. I called Antonio 3 times and got no answer. I started to get worried so I called CJ, he didn't answer either. I paced around the room and thought of every possible reason they would have not to answer. None of the were good. I fought off the thoughts of him getting killed or hurt. I especially hoped the cops weren't questioning them about me. I sat staring at the phone for 30 more minutes until Antonio finally called me.

"Baby! Is something wrong why aren't you answering?"

"Listen baby. I'm fine, but you can't be calling me right now. Stop worrying. Chill out and find something to do. Make me and CJ a big meal. I love you, I'll be home before sun down."

Before I could respond he hung up. He didn't sound fine. He never shut me out like this before. I tried not to worry while I made dinner. I put on music and turned it all the way up. I made fried and grilled chicken, asparagus, mash potatoes, greens, macaroni, bread sticks and lasagna. I even made brownies and cake. It took me three hours. I talked and sung to the baby. She went crazy in my stomach. We ate 3 plates and fell asleep on the couch.

I heard a car door slam after a few hours but I was too tired to get up. About five minutes later Antonio and CJ were walking through the door, talking about something. Antonio came and laid next me and kissed me until I woke up. I tried to push him away but he wouldn't budge.

"Wake up baby."

I turned over and got ambushed by kisses. I opened my eyes slowly and kissed him back.

"Mm. Finally."

"You missed me?"

"Yeah baby. What happened?"

"Don't worry about that baby, everything is taken care of."

CJ came across the room and sat next to me on the couch.

"What's up Preggy."

He said jokingly, putting his arm over me. I looked up at Antonio and he was staring back at me.

"Nothing much." I said sliding from under him, standing up. "I made a bunch of food, so you two better be hungry."

CJ got up immediately and went into the kitchen. I sat back down next to Antonio and grabbed his hand.

"Talk to me. What happened today?"

"Everybody believed my story and said they knew I would be taking over. I have so much power and money it's crazy."

He got up and told me to follow him to the car. He popped the trunk. There was a safe with gold bars, stacks of money and files. He had guns laid out across the trunk and every drug you could think of inside duffel bags.

"I have to distribute this to my workers. I'm going to be going into town often."

He paused for a moment. We moved over to the front patio and he took my hand.

"Baby… They arrested your uncle a few days ago, since he worked for the government he got caught. He was charged with kidnapping, child endangerment and fraud. My love he…"

Antonio paused again and I could feel my heart dropping. I didn't say a word, I just watched him struggle to let the words come out his mouth.

"A while after he was admitted into jail… He um, he killed himself."

I stared at him with a blank face as I felt every part of my heart shatter.

"When I went by your house I saw them taking stuff out. It's a crime scene now. They're looking for you. I went to talk to Kylah and she said they'd taken Angela for questioning, she promised she didn't tell her that you ran. I know she knows the truth about everything but right now I don't think she's a problem. If she starts digging, you know I have to take care of her. I know Kylah is your best friend. But I told her if she gets questioned she needed to be very careful about what she said."

I heard everything he was saying but nothing registered. I couldn't force a tear out of my eye and I couldn't move or respond.

"Martin is still missing but I think he's gone. I know it's a lot to take in, but baby we're going to get through this together. I'm not taking orders anymore, we have unlimited resources, whatever you want or need baby I got you. I'll even let CJ keep you company when I'm gone. He's still my dealer but I know you like him."

He pushed my hair back.

"Are you listening."

I shook my head yes. He pulled me close to him and kissed the top of my head. After a while he picked me up and took me back into the house. CJ was on the couch smoking, eating and watching tv, at the same time loading guns. While Antonio took me upstairs I tried to think, but I couldn't. My mind felt like it was filled with fog. He put me on the bed and laid down next to me, silently running his fingers through my hair.

I turned my head to look at the window and saw a drop of rain fall on it. I closed my eyes and listened to the raindrops fall one after the other.

"It is rain. It's always been the rain." I thought to myself.

I could feel the uneasiness of Antonio as he shifted in bed when the rain began to pour.

"We're having a girl."

The room fell silent and the rain was blocked out.

"I wish things were different." Antonio said, voice cracking with every word. "But I'm happy. You and my little girl will continue to be happy."

Our lives carried on with the same routine. Antonio was cold and distant sometimes when work wasn't going too well. Since he and CJ developed a relationship, he was able to remind him that he was here, with me and our beautiful baby girl.

After I had the baby we decided to name her April. The only true innocence either of us had in our life. She's the one who started my journey in the first place. Antonio was great to her. We traveled in the early years of her life, but I never had the guts to return to Tampa. Kylah and I sent letters back and forth through Antonio.

A few years later when April was walking, Antonio and I got used to life. I graduated high school and CJ decided to live in our guest house, I was finally starting to feel at ease and come to terms with my new life.

Antonio was out in Tampa for the weekend so I decided to take April out of town with me, show her more than the many walls of our cabin. We went to a small town, one smaller than ours, Kindle FL. Walking through the mall, April fell in love with a dress inside the children's store. She ran inside before I even saw her looking. Chasing after her, I bumped into a man that scooped her up. He turned around and smiled.

"Hello pretty girls."

My heart jumped out of my chest.

"Come here baby girl. Come here April."

I reached out for her but she shook her head no and clung to him tighter, he laughed and patted her back.

"What can you say, a girl loves her grandfather."

CPSIA information can be obtained
at www.ICGtesting.com
Printed in the USA
BVOW08*1055090118
504831BV00005B/36/P